A LIVING SOUL

P C Jersild

A LIVING SOUL

TRANSLATED BY RIKA LESSER

Norvik Press
1988

Published titles:

Michael Robinson: *Strindberg and Autobiography*
Irene Scobbie (ed.): *Aspects of Modern Swedish Literature*
Egil Tornqvist and Barry Jacobs: *Strindberg's Miss Julie: a Play and its Transpositions.*
Sigbjørn Obstfelder: *A Priest's Diary,* edited and translated by James McFarlane
Annegret Heitmann (ed.): *No Man's Land* – an anthology of Danish women writers
Bjørg Vik: *An Aquarium of Women,* translated by Janet Garton
Hjalmar Söderberg: *Short Stories,* selected and translated by Carl Lofmark

Forthcoming titles:

James McFarlane: *Ibsen and Meaning: Studies, essays and prefaces 1953–87*
Robin Young: *Time's Disinherited Children. Childhood, Regression and Sacrifice in the Plays of Henrik Ibsen*

Our logo is based on a drawing by Egil Bakka (University of Bergen) of a Viking ornament in gold foil, paper thin, with impressed figures (size 16 x 21 mm). It was found in 1897 at Hauge, Klepp, Rogaland, and is now in the collection of the Historisk museum, University of Bergen (inv.no.5392). It depicts a love scene, possibly (according to Magnus Olsen) between the fertility god Freyr and the maiden Gerðr; the large penannular brooch of the man's cloak dates the work as being most likely 10th century.

Original title: *En levande själ.* © P.C. Jersild, 1980. First published by Albert Bonniers Förlag AB, Stockholm.
This translation © Rika Lesser, 1988.

Cover design: Bob Mason

British Library Cataloguing in Publication Data
Jersild, P.C., 1935–
A Living Soul.
I. Title II. En levande själ. *English*
839.7'374 [F]

ISBN 1-870041-09-7

First published in 1988 by Norvik Press, University of East Anglia, Norwich, NR4 7TJ, England

Managing Editors: James McFarlane and Janet Garton

Norvik Press has been established with financial support from the University of East Anglia, the Danish Ministry for Cultural Affairs, the Norwegian Cultural Department, and the Swedish Institute. Publication of this book has been aided by a grant from the Swedish Institute.

Printed in Great Britain by the University of East Anglia, Norwich.

Translator's Note

While this English rendition (*A Living Soul*) does not essentially differ from the Swedish original (*En levande själ*), some textual surgery has been performed. All the minor excisions, transplantations and implantations have been executed in consultation with the author.

Rika Lesser

Other translations available of works by P.C. Jersild

The Animal Doctor (Djurdoktorn), translated by David Mel Paul and Margareta Paul. Pantheon, New York 1975.

After the Flood (Efter floden), translated by Løne Thygesen Blecher and George Blecher. Morrow, New York 1986.

Children's Island (Barnens ö), translated by Joan Tate, University of Nebraska Press, Lincoln and London 1986.

House of Babel (Babels hus), translated by Joan Tate. University of Nebraska Press, Lincoln and London 1987.

1

Mealtime. I see the girl approaching between the overladen lab benches. For a moment she disappears behind the carboy, a white container that holds distilled water. Now she's coming right at me. She's wearing a green, ankle-length lab coat, a mask of moulded plastic, and a terribly unbecoming crepe-paper cap. The cap is full, gathered at the edge, pulled down to her eyebrows. It looks like a bathing cap from the twenties. Her hands are sheathed in prepowdered rubber gloves and crossed over her bosom. She pushes the gleaming steel lab-cart with her stomach. A green cloth is draped over the flasks and bottles on the lab-cart.

I can only see straight ahead of me. When she reenters my field of vision, she is standing very close by. She bends down to look for something. Then she seizes a long pair of tongs and takes the lid off the aquarium. She squats down in front of the aquarium and looks. I make a mental note that she's got green and silver eyeshadow on today.

The girl busies herself with the glassware on the lab-cart. With a pipette she sucks up some pink fluid. My breakfast. She inserts the pipette into the open aquarium and lets my breakfast drip over me. After a few minutes have passed, I feel breakfast take effect. This is the best time of the day for me, when she bends over me and pours new strength into me. After administering the nutrient solution, she empties four additional, smaller pipettes into my aquarium. I assume they contain vitamins and trace elements, zinc above all. Zinc makes one intelligent. Once all this is done, she checks the oxygen supply and the bath temperature. For the third time she thrusts her face quite close to me, and with her surgical-glove-clad index finger she gently raps on the aquarium. A thrill of sensual pleasure runs through the fluid I rest in.

Now I'm waiting for the round to get here. The aquarium is in a fume hood, so I have a reasonably good view. The laboratory is no larger than an ordinary living room. Two lab benches divide the room into three lanes. Rat cages are piled high against the wall directly opposite me. Somewhat to their right I can glimpse a dog in profile. It's a beagle, suspended by broad straps that gird its stomach. Red tubes dangle from the dog's gut. Juice that resembles glycerine drips from the tubes into small flasks.

My sense of time ebbs and flows like the tides. Sometimes I dream myself into other times, other worlds. Then time passes very quickly. Generally it goes by very slowly. I stare dead ahead and always have the same things in view: the rat cages, the dog, the lab benches cluttered with glassware, the pipes to the emergency shower that is at the left edge of my field of vision. One of the doors to the lab is located next to the shower. The other is somewhere in the background, but so far to the right that I've never seen it. But I know it's there. When the girl leaves the room, she always vanishes towards the right. I take it for granted that she leaves the room. Otherwise she would have to stand pressed against the window seat from four in the afternoon until seven the next morning, when she brings my breakfast. There are also windows to the right. I've never seen them either. But when the sun shines on them, ribbed shadows of venetian blinds and rhombic fields of light travel slowly over the walls. I feel like I'm in the centre of a medieval astrolabe.

The round! Because I'm in water I can't hear a thing, and so I'm always caught napping, so to speak, when the round arrives. Three individuals in white coats suddenly appear in my field of vision: an older man, a middle-aged woman, and a young man. I've christened them the professor, the associate professor, and the postdoctoral student. Oh, how I long for them to linger here with me. I compete with the dog directly opposite for their time. The professor wears no mask. Thus, his is the only face that is entirely naked. He's always tanned a dark bronze. His face has deep lines, his features inspire trust. The associate professor is pale as milk and sports her mask like a tent pitched on the tip of her nose. The postdoc wears his up under his eyes. At least he hasn't got a bathing cap, like the girl who takes care of me.

The professor smiles encouragingly. His teeth are capped. His grey eyebrows, bristly as a moustache, give his face an air of mild surprise. Now he is talking to the others. Greedily, I try to snap up a few words; by now I'm quite good at lipreading, but he turns sideways. I cannot see the replies of the others because of their masks.

Today the round stops for about 30 seconds. I always keep track of time by counting one thousand and one, one thousand and two, one thousand and three . . . The professor nods again and all three of them march briskly over to the beagle. They always spend a long time fussing over the dog, which makes me jealous. They stand and crouch around the dog. Sometimes he gets anxious at night. The lights are never switched off here, so one is compelled to see everything. When the dog gets excited, the tubes can slip out of position. Last night the dog was upset between midnight and two. The girl is summoned and given her instructions.

Just as the round leaves the room and I'm about to take my morning nap to help pass the time, something unusual happens. The girl comes back to me, lugging a medium-sized, rectangular mirror. Carefully she lifts it into the hood and puts it in front of me. But it's far from perpendicular, all I can see is the ceiling. Inside the top of the hood are a fan and a bunch of multi-coloured, intertwined electrical wires. When she moves the mirror I can follow the connections down to my aquarium. On the lid are double rows of banana plugs.

Now she holds the mirror to the vertical and I come into the picture. Hardly an uplifting sight. To speak of a face would be an overstatement. I am a naked brain floating in an aquarium. They have left me one of my eyes. Like a small, painted egg it sits on its stem in front of the brain proper. They have removed everything I have no use for: body, neck, face, cranium, eye muscles. But they have let me keep one eye. I see well - albeit only dead ahead. For some reason they've also left me my outer ears. They droop mournfully, one on either side of the yellowish-grey, convoluted hemispheres of the brain. Deep inside the ears lie the organs of equilibrium - but I can't figure out what I'm supposed to do with my outer ears here in the water. Maybe they function as stabilizers, like fins or keels. To sum up, I look like a gelatinous medusa with long filaments and one gaping enamel eye up in front.

When I see my own reflection, I get sick to my stomach. It's hard for me to accept that I look as I do. But I try to persuade myself to feel happy. After all, when one has long sloshed about in uncertainty, an external identity comes as a great gift. An appearance.

2

What good are our bodies anyway? Legs for example: their sole purpose is transportation. They're a relic from our nomadic existence, when we followed herds of reindeer across Ice Age tundras. And arms? They're a throwback to our time in the flatcrowns on the borders of African savannas. Once you'd plucked a tree bare, it was simply a matter of getting over to the next one: creeping, climbing, hanging, swinging. The body's a construct from the Stone Age, the Bone Age.

The entire world is held in the space of a single human brain. But that brain requires a lot of fancy equipment for its life support system. And the brain itself has obligations for its upkeep, gets mortgaged in the bargain. Enormous capacity is needed to control muscles, respiration, digestion, reproduction, temperature, and numerous other matters of no concern to me. Only a small part of the brain is left for the 'I' itself. I'd wager that my essential core – that which is my real self - weighs somewhere between 200 and 300 grams, in other words, no more than an ordinary parcel of printed matter. In order to support this little package, the average person needs a body weighing 70 kilos.

To keep me going requires nothing but a couple of 1.5-volt batteries. I consume no more energy than a 20-watt bulb. The aqueous solution in which I rest has to be absolutely sterile. Otherwise moss can start to grow on me. The temperature cannot be allowed to vary more than a couple of degrees. If it gets too high my imagination can run wild, too low and I become comatose.

How do I know all this? I who don't even know my name, my age - my sex? That last question may be of minimal interest in the present circumstances. How can I know this? The answer: when they amputated my body, nearly one kilogram of brain tissue - which formerly was occupied with banal body functions - was set free. By using this liberated tissue purely for intellectual activity, I can count on becoming at least five times as intelligent as the average person. Roughly calculated, that comes to an intelligence quotient of 600.

Furthermore, in principle, I can live forever. An ordinary brain grows old and dies owing to poor blood supply. My major blood vessels are gone. They've been extracted with forceps, just as bones are removed from a salmon. Instead of blood, a fluid kept at body temperature oozes through my canals and cavities. Still, I'm not completely immersed. In my ventricles - the innermost hollows of the brain - I've retained some air. That enables me to raise or lower myself in the aquarium.

I consider it an exaggeration to speak of eternal life. Even with perfect care, a calamity must occur someday. Someone can drop the aquarium, or lightning strike the electrical system. So I don't count on eternal life. But practically speaking, I can think in terms of surviving 800 years. Somewhat more than my own IQ. By giving me electric shock treatments, they've disposed of my memory. Thus the greatest threat does not come from outside. Since I've been deprived of all points of orientation, I must steadfastly cling to what little remains. Night and day I'm on tenterhooks. If a single stitch in my fabric goes, anyone at all can unravel me in one long thread.

3

Time for the round. They've already been with me for several minutes. I can see the dog begin to lose patience. The post-doctoral student has fetched a chair for the professor. He's sitting right in front of me, hands on his knees, staring. I stare back at him - what else am I to do? Now the female associate professor is handing him a piece of paper. He reads it several times. Then he gives it to the student, who holds it up in front of me. I read:

> *I, the undersigned, in the presence of witnesses, do hereby affirm that wholly of my own free will, I give my permission and assign and convey into the custody and care of Biochine Medical Corp. my cerebrum, cerebellum, brain stem, and all cerebral nerves appended thereto.*
>
> *With my hand on the pen:*

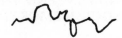

Yes, I remember! The one thing I do recall from my former life: I lay in a respirator. Every day a psychiatrist came to talk to me. After many sessions I accepted the situation. I would never be able to leave the respirator. Year out and year in it would

15

continue to pump air into my lungs. But eventually my body would spurn the machine. My lungs would grow hard and leathery. Finally my heart would stop beating. Such was my situation when a proposal was put before me: let us dispense with your body. That which is *you* resides in your brain. Keeping the brain alive requires neither body nor respirator.

For weeks the psychiatrist and I discussed this. I blinked 'yes' after only a few sessions. But they wanted to convince themselves. The conversations went on interminably. They can hardly be called conversations: the psychiatrist spoke and I blinked. I was ready and willing to do anything in order to escape the iron lung. Lawyers were summoned. The Commission on Ethics was called into special session. Contracts were drawn and redrawn. This is all I can remember. The sharpshooters have done away with all my other memories, discharging electricity from their small-bore, well-aimed tools - a form of shock treatment, caustic and precise. So precise that I still have language, among other things.

Over and over again I read the illegible signature, my mark. I want to know my name, but I cannot decipher it. Finally the student removes the contract by which I surrender myself to Biochine Medical Corp. The professor takes a pad of paper from the associate professor, puts it on his knees and writes. Then he hands the page to the student, who presses it up against the glass of the aquarium:

WE NOW INTEND TO REMOVE THE LAST VESTIGE
OF YOUR MEMORY. GOOD LUCK!

No,no! I want to cry out. Don't blot out the last of me! I tear at my moorings. I try to catch the dog's glance. Of course they can see that I'm getting excited. I'm not so stupid that I don't know what all these wires are for. They've connected me to an electro-encephalograph. As soon as I get upset, it can be traced in the EEG-curves. The professor motions for the associate professor to come forward. She has a small pipette filled with

16

clear, blue fluid. Before my wide-open eye the blue drops trickle down and disperse.

Ten seconds later I feel only gratitude. I've got nothing against starting over. Since they've done away with my happy memories, they're equally welcome to obliterate the bad ones. As soon as he sees that the drops have taken effect, the professor rises from his chair. The postdoc pushes it aside. Then all three of them stand before me. The professor raises his hand and waves.

4

It feels as though the whole summer - is it summer? - is raining away out there. Grey rain batters the glass. When the wind blows hard, I picture small streams of water twitching and being pressed flat against the windowpanes. Even if I could, I have no desire to venture out on to the balcony to see what the weather is doing. I can't manage to stay awake, but I'm not drowsy enough to fall asleep.

The outside world gives me feelings of intense nausea. If I still had eyelids, I would refuse to open them. Now my eye is working round the clock, like a closed-circuit security camera. Of course, one does not have to see if one does not want to. I can whirl around in my swivel chair, turn my back to reality's images, get up on my feet and go - journeying within. One is well-advised not to have inordinate expectations of one's inner landscape. A brain is as bald and hilly as a rocky island in the North Atlantic. Traces of greenery can be found only in the deepest furrows - except for a spot where a few anaemic aspens stand. The wind blowing through their leaves sounds like a tap left running. There are no colours. Everything but the dough-white sun is greyish-grey. For that matter, the whole brain looks like an ambitious but unbaked bread, a fissured and dolled up plaster cast loaf from some regional crafts museum whose subsidies have been frozen.

What kinds of new fluids have they given me today? Stripped naked, utterly defenceless, I am easy prey for the body's juices. Of course, my own body fluids are gone. Those I am exposed to are synthetic imitations, sharp-edged, garish chemicals with artificial fruit flavours.

Am I depressed or just seeing things as they are? No EEG-curves can answer that question. It's like being weary of living. I believe they are experimenting with two different juices, one of them black, the other grey.

The black fluid, the black bile, forces me to fall down a deep, cold, coal-black chasm. One falls and falls without ever hitting bottom and killing oneself - which would be an inestimable relief. When they introduce the black fluid, it's like being put in irons. There is just the one refrain - try to break out: take your own life. But one doesn't even have the energy to fight for it. The black bile washes down and over the soul like an oil spill. All through the night it goes on. By dawn the brain's convolutions are clogged with tar, black seaweed, and dying birds.

No, today they've poured only the grey juice into the soul's bath. The grey depression is no chasm into which one plummets. Rather, it is a bald summit one is compelled to climb. One can see for miles through the clouds of smoke. The landscape is stony, mute, and endless. There are no variations whatsoever, only repetitions. Things close at hand stand out with brazen clarity. Stones in the ground are nauseous; the white fleck in a nail grows overly distinct, obtrusive, and hateful. In the grey depression time stands still. Nothing takes place, not even anxiety.

When the substance begins to leave my system, usually after about four hours, I find myself in the throes of an overpowering desire for colour. I long mainly for yellow and red. Do colours contain vitamins? I wish someone would set the immersion heater's thermostat on maximum. Boil me, coagulate me so that I'll shimmer yellow and red as a lobster!

I am so sunken in my own melancholy that I haven't noticed that the associate professor-psychiatrist has come into the laboratory. She has a girl with her, one I've never seen before. The girl is lugging a tray loaded with racks of test tubes, small

19

flasks, pipettes, plastic syringes, and various other disposable items. First they take samples of the fluid in which I rest, sucking up centilitre draughts which they dump into various test tubes. The tubes are carefully coded with secret numerical combinations.

Then the girl puts on a pair of rubber gloves, moves her hands down into the aquarium, and cautiously but firmly encircles me with them, as one holds a fruit that damages easily. Meanwhile the psychiatrist works with a glistening instrument, equipped with a shining needle that is roughly 25 centimetres long. I don't feel a thing. A brain cannot feel physical pain. They could even sliver me slowly with a cheese-slicer without my screaming. Now they're just taking a couple of puncture samples; infinitesimal bits of my tissue are sucked up into the long needle.

5

The hands of the wall clock point to seven; punctually the girl enters the scene from the right of my field of vision. She passes the distilled water carboy and turns to face me. Hands crossed over her chest, as usual, she pushes the lab-cart with her stomach - as usual. But her face is not the same as usual: *she is not wearing a mask!* My heart pounds violently . . . of course it's not my heart that's beating; after all it's been severed with the rest of my body. But if one can still have feelings in a leg that's been amputated, obviously one can feel a lost heart. It all goes on in the brain anyway - everything.

There is nothing remarkable about her face. Because of that cap that looks like a piece of waxed paper held on the top of a preserves jar with a rubber band, I can't see her forehead; and if she hadn't blacked them in with pencil, her eyebrows, too, would be invisible. Now that they are no longer alone in her face, her grey-green eyes have lost a certain degree of intensity. With the mask gone, a thin nose, a large, thick-lipped mouth, and two childishly pouting cheeks detract from them.

When she leans towards me I become quite hot. The next moment I get scared. Shouldn't she really be wearing a mask over her mouth?! Has she simply forgotten it? In that case, right now I am being exposed to the risk of deadly infection. Some microorganisms, entirely harmless to normal people, can extricate themselves from her saliva, sail over the aquarium, drop down through the opening for the immersion heater, and begin to circulate. In that case, in a matter of hours they will invade me and take root in me, like nettles on a virgin dung heap.

But she calms me down. She must have noticed the fear in my eye. Her big, orange-coloured mouth smiles at me while she runs her index finger around it. She wants to call my attention to the absent mask; to show this is not a case of neglect, but rather something done with the professor's consent. I become a bit cross with myself; I should have been able to figure out from the very first that she's not dangerous without her mask. After all, for as long as I can remember, the professor has not worn one. Professors can scarcely be less perilous carriers than lab assistants.

One of her front teeth is crooked. She closes her mouth, waves with her fingertips, and repairs to the meal-cart. My stomach is rumbling. She sucks up some pink fluid in the large pipette. I shut my eyes and enjoy myself, imagining lying at my mother's breast. While she lets the beads of fluid nutrients down into the aquarium, I wonder: my mother? Did I have a mother? Or have I been born here in the research lab - in an incubator?

Soon I've had my fill and am given my vitamins and trace elements. While I digest my food, she props her elbows up on the base of the hood, bends forward, and looks at me full of expectation. Never before have we been so close to each other. What I miss most right now about my body is my teeth. One cannot smile without teeth. How can I make her understand? My only remaining movable body parts are my drooping outer ears. I try to find the nerves to my ear muscles, but I'm rusty. I'm like a boxer who has been too long out of the ring. Was I ever capable of wiggling my ears? I don't dare go on: if I suddenly get my ears going fast, with a couple of swift strokes I could drive my naked eye smack into the wall of the aquarium.

First of all there's something I want to know: what my name is. I concentrate on the question: w-h-a-t i-s m-y n-a-m-e??? She looks a bit taken aback, as if hearing a very distant sound, a scarcely audible cricket. Then she leans even closer. W-h-a-t i-s m-y n-a-m-e????? Her lips begin to grope for words. I'm

not at all confident about my lipreading, but now I am certain:
- Whwhwhwhtttt. Whaaa . . . What? her lips say.
- I-s m-y n-a-m-e????
- Iiiiii-ssssss . . . mmmmyyyy . . . nnnnaaaa-me!
It works! Thought transference functions. And I, who always -
always? - have suspected anything coming under the rubric of
the sixth sense.

She laughs somewhat distractedly, she is happy. Together we
have found something, we have discovered parts of our senses
we did not believe existed. Then she leans very close indeed, so
near that I'm afraid she'll smear lipstick on the aquarium. Her
lips form a kiss.

I grow warm again. Not on the top of my head, but further
down, in the mass beneath it, and in the stump of my medulla
oblongata. But I don't want a kiss. I want an answer. What is
my name?

It is not a kiss, it is the beginning of a word - a name - that
looks like a kiss. What letter of the alphabet looks like a kiss
when uttered? A, B, C, D . . . The answer is Y. After the Y
comes a little puff of air . . . P! Making the next sound, she
bares her teeth . . . S! Then she grimaces, as if she'd stuck her
foot in ice-cold water . . . I!
- Ypsilon, she's saying.

I'm a little surprised. I had imagined I went by a number, a
series of numerals. But I've also assumed that the personnel
here have a nickname for me. Why not 'The Blob'? Or 'The
Genius'?

My name is Ypsilon. Ypsilon is the twentieth letter of the
Greek alphabet. Quite a chic name, a name that has a distinct
ring of statesmanship. But I'm not a complete idiot: if they've
christened me with a letter of the alphabet, there's a distinct
implication that there have been an Alpha, a Beta, a Gamma,
and so forth, before me. No fewer than nineteen others - what
has become of them? Were they failures? Did they coagulate?
Did they wear out? Did my nineteen predecessors get poured
down the drain?

23

- Ypsilon, she repeats, grinning.

I know, I know. Now I want to know: how old am I? Where did you get me from . . . No, don't go away! She moves backwards, waves, and turns her back on me. Wait!! I try to think straight through her back: what is *your* name?! Now she leaves quickly with the lab-cart. Most likely it's time to make coffee for the research team. I lie for a long time before the surface of the liquid in the aquarium is calm once again.

6

It is night-time. Only the dog is awake. A strap under his chin has come loose. The dog lowers his head and glares at me. Froth slobbers from his flabby lips. What is he thinking about? Food? The dog no longer has any use for his mouth and teeth. Nourishment enters his stomach directly through a tube. Does the dog understand what he sees when he looks at me? A pale yellow bundle of knots in a shimmering green aquarium - how does the world around me construe me? I wish the dog were unleashed at night. They could put a table in front of my tank, and he could lie on it, paws tucked under his chin. One eye trained on me, the other watching the door. Now and then the dog would get up, stretch, yawn, nose the aquarium, wag his tail, and lick the glass.

Maybe we could get out of here together. How long can I be without water? Some canine breeds have a soft bite - how soft? Would it be possible for the dog to stick his muzzle down in here very carefully and take me in his mouth? As a puppy is carried. And once we are outside, I must quickly be lowered into the nearest pool of water. And then? Actually, I can move of my own accord. Lately I've gained far greater control over my outer ears. Beating them in time with each other, I could plough ahead like a little paddle steamer. But if my ears aren't synchronized, I'll go around in circles until all my strength is gone.

I succeed in fixing the dog's gaze on me. Immediately he raises his head and pricks up his ears. His lower jaw falls and his tongue spills out. I concentrate to my utmost. Since I can convey messages to the girl via thought transference, it ought to work with the dog. Can dogs talk - or think? What shall I say to the dog - Fetch!? Give me a sign, I think. Bark, whimper, yap! Hanging there, the dog grows uneasy. His legs run, the tubes dangle and sway. He wrinkles his nose, shows his teeth, and makes a lunge for the nearest tube. A success. The tube breaks and quivers. What have I done?! I think as hard as I can: Nice doggie, nice bowwow . . . quiet now. The dog lets go of the tube, hangs his head, and pants. Afraid of being thrashed, he gives me one of those pitifully furtive looks.

Do I dare make another attempt? I must know whether I'm getting through to the dog, or if what just happened was mere chance. Again I seek out his gaze, switch on the hypnosis and think: What a nice paw! Give me that paw! The dog tries to evade my glance, but I don't relent: Nice paw! Give me that paw! The dog's right paw begins to twitch. It is raised and goes higher. It scratches aimlessly in the empty air. Then he starts to lick it. Long licks that become more and more rapid. Finally, this licking takes on an almost indecent character.

7

The soul resides between the lines in the brain. Perhaps the web of brain tissue itself is unnecessary. Then the soul would be a free-floating force field. Can Darwin answer the question, how many billions of years would such an evolutionary step require? Until now the soul has been thought of as a magnetic field. To hold the field in place and in balance, there have to be poles, brain cells.

One thinks quite a lot when one has nothing to do but lie around. Can it serve any purpose? They have set up three oscilloscopes on the lab bench so I can monitor my condition. An oscilloscope looks like a narrow, sheet-metal box with a little window, like a TV-screen. Inside it, curves of light shimmer against a green background. If I suffer an intense emotion, the curves begin to throb in the oscilloscopes. When I lie here idling, they flatten into nearly straight lines.

I have named the three oscilloscopes, in order, from top to bottom: ANGRY, SATISFIED, and LONGING.

Simplifications, to be sure. ANGRY responds to all conditions of agitation, not solely rage. SATISFIED doesn't just show when my stomach is full; SATISFIED gauges well-being in the wider sense of the word. It is LONGING I have most difficulty coming to terms with. Sometimes LONGING erupts without my understanding why.

When the research team came by today, they connected me to a fourth piece of equipment; I think its name is CLEVER. One after another they filed in: first the professor, then the associate professor with a looseleaf binder under her arm, and last the postdoc lugging a big crate. In the crate lay CLEVER. CLEVER consists of one red and one green light mounted in a console. Next to them sits a small glass container of blue fluid. Thin tubing runs over to my aquarium. Every time the green lamp lights, the container dispenses a drop of blue fluid. Instantaneously I am in the grips of overwhelming bliss. I fancy I am ruling the world.

They tested CLEVER a few times. Each time they did, I went straight up into the heavens like a rocket, and each time I plummeted back down, always landing head-first in the clay. Before they went on to the dog, the professor leaned into the hood, tapped against my glass tank, smiled and said very distinctly:

- Clever, clever . . .

8

There's no doubt about it, I have only one eye. And yet, when the girl came in this morning it felt as if I had two. Spying with one of them, I took in her entrance, her vanishing briefly behind the distilled water container, and finally her head-on approach to my aquarium in a slow triumphal march. My other eye was glued to the bottom oscilloscope, LONGING. As soon as I caught sight of her, the activity in LONGING died down. Maybe that explains why personal encounters always seem best before they actually transpire.

She never wears a mask any more. Instead of being unequivocally glad about this, I spend the better part of the day lying around hoping she'll take off her bathing cap.

- Good morning, Ypsilon, she says. Did you have a good night?

I do not tell her what's really on my mind, about my longing, my threadbare fantasies, about my fear of the rats and my concern for the dog - instead of trying to convey all this via thought transference, I make a couple of scarcely perceptible strokes with my outer ears, curtsey prettily, bow gracefully. Maybe I'm underestimating her, maybe it's a misconception that girls are scared away by too much candour when a relationship is only beginning.

Our morning hours of dalliance have been considerably prolonged these last weeks. She no longer feeds me absent-mindedly, as when one tosses a few herrings to the seals. We chat a little about the wind and the weather before the actual feeding - and when the feeding is over, she gets herself a stool, a plastic cup, and a jar of instant coffee, then fills her cup with hot water from the tap in the hood. Then she sits down, leaning her elbow into the hood. I see her in profile when she drinks. Between gulps of coffee she looks straight into my eye; we practise thought transference and lipreading respectively. I always ask her to get as close to me as possible. Not because I'm especially nearsighted, but because in this way she blocks out the equipment on the bench behind her. It's distracting to have to read off one's emotional life in the oscilloscopes all the time.

We usually begin by limbering up a little. You see, she is rather sleepy in the mornings, particularly in the lips. Her eyes are awake but her mouth is not. The tongue and the lips must do careful calisthenics to get going properly. If we overdo the exercises, she begins to slur her words and everything becomes incomprehensible. If everything becomes incomprehensible, I get upset. And when I get upset, the uppermost oscilloscope, ANGRY, reacts - and that's the end of our tête-à-tête.

- What is your name? she begins according to schedule.
- My name is Ypsilon. The twentieth letter of the Greek alphabet. And what is your name?
- Mmmmmmm-a!

We always laugh at that. It is our private joke, the foundation of our intimacy.

- Is your name really Mamma? I thought transfer to her.
- Emmm-mmma! she clarifies.
- I love Emma!

She laughs so hard at this that she nearly spills her coffee. With every day that passes she laughs harder and harder. Things are beginning to get serious between us.

Once a week I get a bath. I've stabilized myself now and can leave my sterile aquarium. Emma puts a bucket of body-temperature, distilled water in the hood. Then she carefully sees to the thin wires and the banana plugs. The first minutes are delightful. She holds me in her hands. But when she withdraws her right hand to begin disconnecting me, section after section of my consciousness is extinguished. I become a huge house in which the security guard makes his rounds, turning off the light in room after room. When she lifts me out of the aquarium and puts me into the bucket - she's told me how this is done - by then I'm completely out of it; an inactive, blacked-out mass of eggwhite, with no more human dignity than an omelette.

I would so like to experience the bath from beginning to end. In particular, I would like to know how it feels to come back to a spotless aquarium filled with fresh fluid. It must be like crawling into a bed with newly-ironed, cool sheets. We have talked about this. But Emma says she doesn't dare go against her instructions. Neither of us knows what would happen if I were still hooked up when I was being transferred out of or into the aquarium. There's a chance I would not survive the experience.

When she's gone and I lie there, rinsed clean and waiting, I cannot help pondering over the most recent piece of equipment; I'm talking about CLEVER with its two lamps and container of joy-juice. I can't come up with a better word than joy-juice. I've asked Emma about it, but she doesn't know. She says there's a label pasted to the bottom of the container. Written on the label in red marker is a long chemical formula. She has mouthed the equation to me several times. But she herself knows no chemistry, and here in the aquarium, I suffer from an acute lack of reference works.

I'm a little bit afraid of CLEVER: I can't decide if CLEVER is a threat or a source of joy.

Am I making any headway, in other respects? I believe so. With each day that passes, I venture farther and farther into the labyrinth of the disengaged parts of my brain: those parts, the ganglia, nerve centres, and nuclei which previously were tied to my banal body functions. I wander about quietly and with a light tread. I find myself in a palace, closed for the season. Furniture, painting, spinets, chandeliers, beds, sculptures, windows . . . everything is still draped with white sheets. But

31

one day all the covers will be lifted and everything will be cleaned, dusted off, and come back into use; one day the windows will open onto the park which stands outside. It will be the celebration of the century. In the pond in the palace grounds, a flotilla will launch a display of multicoloured fireworks.

9

This morning they make their rounds several minutes too early. Poor Emma is taken by surprise. Perched on her stool next to the aquarium, she is lost in her knitting. These last few days she's begun to knit while listening to the thoughts I send her. She needs to turn her face up towards me only when she answers. What is she making? It's beginning to look like a tea-cosy. I don't dare inquire. It couldn't possibly be a surprise for yours truly, could it?

I see them coming but don't manage to warn her in time. Not until the professor bumps into the meal-cart does Emma notice them. She darts out to the right, beyond the edge of my field of vision, leaving everything behind her: the coffee mug, the knitting instructions she propped up against the aquarium, and an extra ball of wool. The three figures clad in white stop in their tracks, not really knowing what to do with Emma's things. Finally the postdoc shoves the ball of wool into the topmost pocket of his lab coat, where it is conspicuous, as showy as a breast.

Evidently, they've finally got the rest of the do-it-yourself kit for CLEVER. They attach an output printer to CLEVER. The printer consists of an electric typewriter with a type ball, and a narrow strip of paper that comes out of the short side of the machine. In my vicinity they've set up a photoelectric cell by inserting two metal poles into the aquarium, one at either side, somewhat obliquely in front of my eye. They also provide CLEVER with a large picture-screen, nearly one metre square.

Finally they paste a piece of paper directly on to the aquarium. Not right in front of my eye, but somewhat to the left. I have to cast sidelong glances in order to read the text. It is a Morse alphabet. After the letter A is ·-, after B -··· , after C -·-·, and so forth.

The professor puts his hand into the aquarium and gingerly pushes me forward. First a sharp shove and then a more lingering movement, consequently corresponding to ·-, which is to say, the letter A. I have already understood what he has in mind: with the help of my movable ears I'm expected to advance on command. But how will I be able to retreat? There's a solution to this as well; quite simply, they've stretched a rubber band around the stem of my brain. The elastic is fastened to the back wall of the aquarium. As soon as my ears stop swimming forward, the rubber band draws me back to my starting point.

Now a pale colour image is visible on the screen mounted on top of CLEVER. The picture shows an ape, who is sitting with a half-peeled banana. In the upper left corner of the frame there's a capital A. The professor leans in toward me again, reaches his hand into the aquarium and tickles me lightly over my derrière. When I don't move of my own accord, he gives me a firm shove forward, as if I were a bark boat. But I don't stir a limb. What does he want? What are all these expensive toys for?

I connect my thought transference and think straight into his forehead:

- I would be tremendously grateful if you would explain what all this is for. To what end does Biochine intend to use me? Do you want my opinion of apes, or their diet, or bananas, or about discourtesy toward lab assistants, *or what??*

Thought transference is not working. I make three extremely vigorous attempts. The only result is that he massages his temples, as if feeling the onset of a stress-induced headache.

I lose patience and begin to beat my ears in a frenzy, so that I'm propelled forward, and at irregular intervals I cut off the photoelectric cell - the invisible beam that extends between the

34

two metal poles in front of me. Now and then I'm jerked backward by the elastic band. The electric typewriter begins to work and by fits and starts spews out its paper tape. The associate professor and postdoctoral student hold it up. It reads: $BBGN_3WWQ_{34}$. Exhausted, I lie staring at the strip of paper. I have pains in my ear muscles and, because of the rubber band, in my brainstem as well.

They are all visibly displeased. Not the least CLEVER, whose red lamp begins to blink. They carry out an intelligence test: a small pipette is lowered into the aquarium. They lift it up and examine it. The concave meniscus easily rests at an IQ of 500. Then they give up. I assume they're retiring to the coffee room. Dejected, I lie staring at all the instruments. A miserable morning. I want Emma here with me. Is that what I want? Yes, the curves in the undermost oscilloscope, LONGING, gradually begin to arch their backs: I'm longing . . .

Until now, Emma and I have only tried out thought transference at short distances; I estimate the longest distance at four-tenths of a metre. A thin glass wall, that of the aquarium, doesn't seem to be an obstacle. But what about doors, concrete walls, stairwells - elevators? Even though I'm all tired out after swimming, I exert myself to the utmost and transmit:

- Emma, dearest, come to me!

Then I wait. Patient as a troubadour under a maiden's balcony. Has she heard me? Has someone else heard me? It's not necessarily true that everyone is as unreceptive as the professor. Do I dare to sing another tune . . . yes, I will. Risking the onslaught of all the castle's soldiers.

- Emma, my all, I'm yearning, yearning . . .

The oscilloscope LONGING swerves encouragingly. Emma comes in from the left, out of breath. She has thick gloves on her hands and a rubber apron over her coat. She sticks her head into the hood. She is so irritated that I can scarcely manage to read her lips.

- I was with the rats. What do you want?!

- Your help, Emma.

- With what? I have to see to the rats!
- What do they want, the professor and all the others, what so they want me to do??
- Cooperate.
- How??
- You know that very well yourself! And besides, I have no intention of getting mixed up in it. I'm going back to the rats, now!
- No, no . . . Emma, you're the only person I can depend on.
- Do as they say. Unless you want to go to the psychiatrist! That's the only advice I can give you.

Emma turns on the heels of her clogs and leaves.

- Give my regards to the rats . . . I say, with far too little enthusiasm to give it the strength to penetrate the back of her head.

Unless I want to go to the psychiatrist. Is that a threat or a promise? But I've already seen the psychiatrist. I don't recall the details - but I *know*. Maybe it was in some previous life. At the bottom of the brain, down in the keelson, lies rubbish from another time. Every time my path takes me down there, I shut my eyes and hold my nose.

Old albumen stinks of sulphur. Rising from the heap of discarded memories, an image takes form: a sick-room seen from the bed. My self paralysed, prostrate, incapable of moving anything but my eyes. A woman dressed in black enters, nods in the doorway, takes a chair, sits down beside me, and touches my cheek. I have no feeling in the cheek. But when I glance sideways to the right, I can see her hand.

10

Night-time. A fluorescent lamp in the ceiling flickers and throbs. For a long time it beats steadily, until suddenly a quick rhythmic series is followed by a pause. Each time this happens I think the light will go out for good, like an old person's heart. I cannot sleep. I spend so much of my time idling during the day that I sabotage my night's sleep. Whom shall I ask? Emma's the only person I have a kind of contact with - but she's not authorized to dispense drugs. The question needs to be put to the professor or the associate professor. I have no way of talking to them.

I lie and wait for the dog, hung up in his harness at the other end of the room, to grow restless. His usual periods of uneasiness come between midnight and two. His whole body shakes, his legs take little running steps, as if they were bound with a rubber band; his mouth twitches, and when he really gets going, he bares his teeth. Most often the dog's eyes are half-closed, but sometimes he stares wildly. Nothing to worry about - the dog is dreaming. But the tubes under his stomach can become dislodged. And I don't like it when that happens, because the research team spends so much time readjusting the dog's gear that they barely have time to blow me a kiss.

Tonight the dog is not dreaming. He is every bit as awake as I am and hangs there motionless. Only his ears move now and then, as if shooing away a fly. But there have never been any flies in here. I wonder what the world outside is like. Have I seen it? Does it exist? I assume it exists; otherwise where would Emma go after four p.m.? Maybe the external world does not exist; maybe

Emma, in a gaseous cloud, is transformed into a pixie, hovering among the galaxies until the alarm clock goes off early the next morning.

The three individuals in white coats, the professor *et consortes*, also must have somewhere or other to be for the greater part of the day. Or maybe they just pass into the room adjacent to this one and wait there like wooden dolls - when the bell tolls nine, they march out in file, driven by the works of a medieval clock.

Something's happening!! I'm looking at the dog's back; the dog's back arches as it does only when it's time to defecate in the plastic bag, which is securely fastened under the base of the dog's tail. But it's not time for the dog to empty his bowels. Something is sitting on the dog's back, making him arch it. Something white and pink that moves convulsively. It is a white rat. It is uncommonly large, the body almost as big as a squirrel's. Another one! A big white and pink rat climbs up the dog's suspension frame and seats itself high up on a crossbar. It sits there and looks down. Is it jeering or calling out to its companions? A third and a fourth rat advance from the right. They get up on top of the white carboy of distilled water, stand on their hind legs and greedily breathe the air. A fifth and a sixth and a seventh, nose to tail, scurry along the black edge of the lab bench.

I would like to close my eyes. I would like to close my eyes, shake my head, massage my eyebrows with my fingertips, and pinch myself on the arm: am I dreaming?! Is there something wrong with my fluids, am I suffering from some kind of chemical delirium? But this is no dream. Dreams are elastic; in dreams perspective is stretched or foreshortened. What I'm seeing now is concrete, is consistent in time and space. Nearly a dozen large white rats are invading the laboratory. There may well be an extremely banal explanation for this: someone has failed to close the cage properly.

I feel a twinge in the legs I no longer have. The next moment I'm lame. A rat is climbing in front of me. It sits down about a tenth of a metre away and energetically polishes its nose with its sweet marzipan hands. With half-open mouth and hands halfway raised, it stops and stares at me. Then it gets back into action: assiduously combing back its ears and plastering down its head hairs with water.

A shockwave travels through the solution in which I rest. Someone is on the lid of the aquarium. The rat in front of me is also looking up above me, and both of its paws scratch the empty air. Have they discovered me?! What are they up to: will they call to the others or keep me for themselves? The rat above me runs quickly back and forth. I get a couple of nasty jolts when it pushes past the electrical cords. I have but one wish: that they gnaw through the wires, producing a complete blackout of my inner being before they eat me.

With a brutal splash, I'm heaved over to one side and begin to list to starboard. Outside, the laboratory inclines precariously. I have company in the aquarium. I feel the lash of a whip over one of my ears, and in the next moment a rat comes swimming over me, with its belly hanging down. Its tail beats. The rat seems confused, scrapes the glass, turns, and dives. With its cheeks puffed out and its nostrils pinched together, it glowers straight into my eye.

I must not be afraid! I must not . . . Yes I must!!! I violently let go of all my feelings. Through the turbulent water I see the three oscilloscopes directly opposite; they're fluttering this way and that, as if seen in a curved mirror. Scared! Scared! I have to become even more scared, SCARED, S-C-A-R-E-D!!! At last the instrumentation reacts: when all the curves threaten to derail, the alarm goes off.

Maybe I pass out for a few seconds - or else I'm just seasick. When I regain consciousness, a security guard is standing in front of me, holding a soaking wet rat in his hand. Then the door to the hood is rolled down. There aren't any left in here, are there? Some acrobatic rat, a trapeze artist, hanging with its tail wrapped like a clinging vine around one of the electric cords in the top of the hood?

Half an hour later the associate professor and the postdoctoral student arrive. In the meantime the guard has caught several rats.

Now a systematic hunt is under way. They even climb into the hood and run the beams of their flashlights around inside. I begin to calm down. They are as thorough as customs inspectors.

11

I have been to the psychiatrist. The associate professor is not just
a woman but a psychiatrist as well. All this time she has stood
behind and to one side of the professor, and had his ear like a
second Richelieu.

The associate professor-psychiatrist and I have made only
superficial contact. It's a matter of distrust on my part. As long
as the purpose of my being here in the aquarium is concealed
from me, I can do nothing to open my mind and heart. Why don't
I have memory? Because they have blasted it away with electricity. They must have started from the premise that a brain which
lugs around its past, a trawling net full of experiences, cannot be
efficient. I think they are wrong. I remember nothing - and this
fact takes up 90 per cent of my time; a fruitless searching for a
previous life. I have plans to invent my memoirs, so that once and
for all I can be rid of the problem. But what sort of guarantee do
I have that they won't give me yet another series of electric
shocks, which will destroy my fabricated memory?

When I was in consultation with the psychiatrist, they rolled
down the blinds, as if for a seance. Afterwards they coupled me
to the EEG-machine that detects and records my brain waves.
Then the associate professor-psychiatrist sat down on a stool
obliquely in front of the hood. Before I had time to concentrate
on her high forehead, so as to make an impression on her, she
began to show slides. On the big screen, part of CLEVER's
apparatus, she projected the old, well-known Rorschach inkblots.
Designs which were once made by spilling ink and Indian ink on

paper which was then folded over twice. How do I know this? Have I myself been a psychologist - or a patient? We went through the whole battery of pictures: the butterflies, the thunderclouds, the kidneys, the trees, and the one that looks like the head of an insect magnified 150 times. For each test picture a new EEG-curve was registered.

I felt calm almost the whole time. I know that my innermost self can't be fooled by such coarse conjuror's tricks as electroencephalography. But after half an hour, when I began to feel a bit tired, I was consumed by a nagging anxiety: can I really be sure? Maybe the researchers are far more intelligent than one thinks. Maybe they are systematically pulling the wool over my eyes. Maybe it's all a cunning conspiracy with Emma as a double agent? Maybe the psychiatrist is a common agent provocateur and the professor's smile itself is a Rorschach test image? Maybe . . . there are so many maybe's. If I could have, I would have screamed at the psychiatrist: give me back my past! So long as you leave me wavering here in uncertainty in the aquarium, we won't get anywhere. If you want to extract something from my brain, it will have to be on my own terms! Will it have to be? Isn't this just an invocation, a vain wish on my part, a self-deception, a rigmarole I talk myself into, a futile belief in the freedom of the spirit. One day, when they've sharpened their instruments sufficiently, I will trip along at their heels like a dachshund, or waddle like a duckling imprinted on the first moving object it sees, a cardboard box pulled on a string. I have no more real choice than a transplanted kidney: either we must cooperate or else allow ourselves to be thrust aside, plucked out, and flushed down the drain.

12

Sometimes I itch so desperately between my shoulderblades. *How did I get here?* That's become an obsession with me. Maybe there's a medicine for this, something water soluble? My memory has begun to return. How else can I explain sequences of images from a previous life: faces, surroundings, someone weeping . . . These appearances come through like distant, disruptive interference on TV. As soon as I attempt to fix on these reminiscences, they glide away like motes in the eye.

Take my name, Ypsilon. It feels artificial. I must have been called something else before. Last night, when my gloominess lingered, sharp as the glare from a fluorescent light over the laboratory, I got it into my head that my name is Pavlov. Several times I tried saying 'Pavlov'. But none of the apparatus reacted in the least, not ANGRY, SATISFIED, LONGING - or CLEVER. Therefore I assume that it's a blind alley.

For the rest, I occupy myself a great deal with the Morse code. I learned it immediately from the piece of paper they've pasted down towards the left. I interpret all sorts of signals. The malfunctioning fluorescent tube up there in the ceiling, babbling its gibberish around the clock - can't anyone get that damned thing to shut up! When the weather changes outside, I try to interpret it. A long shadow, a short light, and so forth. When the professor comes in the mornings, he always attempts to establish contact by rapping the nail of his index finger against the aquarium. What is he tapping out? Several times I've understood it as S O S, 'Save Our Souls!'

For a while I believed I had the brain of a child. Not a baby brain, absorbed with its sucking reflexes - I have not at any time felt the least desire to suck on any of the objects in my immediate vicinity, neither on the immersion heater, nor the thermometer, nor the photoelectric cell. If I'm a child, it's likely that I'm somewhere between the ages of ten and twelve. Still somewhat flexible, but with sufficiently long neural pathways to erect abstract constructions in the air. But I believe I am older. My relationship to Emma - she is actually a little over twenty - indicates that I have at least gone through puberty.

My brain is a castle whose inhabitants have withdrawn to one of its wings, living in three rooms and a kitchen. I want to see the castle full of people, I want to see the rooms used, the chimneys working, the whole establishment seething with life, as on the evening before a carnival: a brass ensemble practising in the dining room; barrels being tapped in the cellar; a huge, smiling papier-maché head like a drifting hot-air balloon come to rest on the king-size bed in the master's chamber.

Why should brains be located in the head? If they lay in the breast or in the stomach, their upkeep would be considerably facilitated. Or in the scrotum: warm and cosy, capable of being elevated or lowered as need be. Some species of animals, worms for instance, have brains in both ends. That human beings have chosen to go the centralized way has also left them extremely vulnerable.

The fundamental error is that we seek individual solutions. Several people ought to share one brain. In that case *one* body, the family's fittest, would suffice. A number of unforeseen technical difficulties could arise when several people moved into the same head. The simplest solution would then seem to be to await the natural migratory periods; for humans these are not spring and autumn but death. When a person dies, the foundation for his or her soul is destroyed. Like a poor magpie, the soul is forced to flee and vainly flaps around looking for a new branch to sit on.

In the future human consciousness will come to take widely

divergent forms. Some will establish a collective of souls in those spacious, old luxury apartments, in convoluted art-nouveau brains. Others will settle themselves in plants or animals. But why not, quite simply, in a warmed-up, thoroughly moistened loaf of bread; as bacteria are cultivated in a petri dish filled with broth?

Life in an aquarium seems to be, for the most part, rather stagnant. Am I a ragged goldfish in a pond, or am I the oracle of some god?

13

Biochine's scientific bigwigs, the professor and associate professor among them, have gone off to a congress. Nowadays the post-doctoral student makes the rounds by himself. But he doesn't devote much of his attention to me. He seems to be more interested in the equipment. Vast stretches of the laboratory's interior wall are covered by my speech-strips. He has tacked up in long rows my unsuccessful efforts, my incomprehensible utterances. Under these he has pinned up the EEG-curves, from which one can read the electrical currents in my brain. He can sit and stare for hours at the respective strips, with the same sullen fascination the Egyptologist Champollion once must have bestowed on the Rosetta stone, before he solved the mystery of the hieroglyphs.

The postdoc now seems obsessed with the idea that something is wrong with the equipment. Thus it cannot be I who cannot read, but rather that some part of the machinery is malfunctioning. Yesterday he completely disassembled CLEVER, and not just CLEVER but LONGING as well. It felt odd no longer to be able to register such an important part of my emotional life. I didn't think about Emma even once. To make matters worse, the postdoc did not manage to put the oscilloscope back together, but had to telephone the company for service. Which could not have been cheap since it was three in the morning. But maybe it's all still under guarantee. Am I covered by the guarantee?

We have had exercises in reading. The picture of the banana-eating ape has been shown repeatedly on the screen. But I have consistently declined to signal A via the Morse code. Nor have I chosen to signal the same error each time. Sometimes I signal Q, sometimes Z, and not so seldom a miscellany of letters. All my pronouncements are carefully scrutinized and set up on the wall.

This morning I was treated to a grand surprise. While I lay digesting my breakfast, the round appeared. But the postdoctoral student was not alone. He had a chimpanzee in tow, who, according to Emma, is known hereabouts by the name of Flink. They came marching in file: first the postdoc in his old clogs and with his coat open, as usual - and behind him Flink in his little, specially-tailored coat, neatly buttoned from top to bottom. With his hands behind his back and the deep creases in his forehead, Flink was a carbon copy of the professor. They even have the same complexion.

While the postdoc leaned into the hood and scratched the glass of the aquarium, Flink climbed up and sat himself down on the topmost oscilloscope. There he sat, puffing himself up, as if he were the managing director of all Biochine. Normally Flink lives in the attic, where they have a special ape department. But now he has the run of the place. I assume this is no mere whim of the institute's management, rather that it's some phase in a resocialization programme.

Now Flink has climbed down. He dashes around between the lab benches, with deeply bent knees, like Groucho Marx. He can't keep his hands off anything. One gets such an urge to slap his fingers. The postdoc provides no supervision. On the contrary, he seems to enjoy having the overly inquisitive Flink kicking up a row at his heels.

I've discovered something else that troubles me: the postdoctoral student is not uninterested in Emma. He finds pretexts to be with her. And now, this afternoon, he has bought some cake to go with the coffee. He and Emma sit at the farther end of the long bench with their plastic mugs and their slit-open, flattened-out paper cups, which they use as cake plates. They've hung a newspaper over the frame in which the dog is suspended so that he cannot see the cake slices. If the dog sees something tasty, he produces so much gastric juice that the experiment he is involved in could be jeopardized. Flink was given some cake straight away, so that he would leave the other two in peace. So now he is crouching in the opening to the hood, blocking my view, my surveillance. His broad mouth grins right in front of my face. His long fingers pluck at the air. But mostly he chatters. Flink has learned several hundred signs in sign language. His larynx is so constructed as to make speech, in the ordinary sense of the word, impossible. On the other hand, he belongs to the rapidly growing band of sign-language-speaking apes, whose most famous representative is Koko the female gorilla.

It is far simpler for me to read Flink's signs than to interpret the postdoc's sloppy lip-slurring. But unfortunately, Flink has little of interest to say. A pity. As things now stand, it is only from Emma that I can get information. Flink could have become an excellent addition, if he weren't so frightfully taken up with his own importance, if the majority of what he says were not practically word-for-word repetitions of what the professor says when he makes his rounds. But worst of all: he is sitting in my way! What are the postdoc and Emma up to over there?! Now they are even smoking - which is strictly forbidden in the lab!

Flink's coconut head rocks back and forth; suddenly he asks:

- Why don't you cooperate?!
- Go to hell! I say via thought transference.

For a moment Flink looks utterly perplexed and clutches his round forehead. So the message got through. I myself become a little bit overexcited - until now, only Emma and possibly the dog have received my telepathic communications. I get so overexcited that ANGRY sounds the alarm. At once the postdoc comes shuffling over to where we are. First he looks at ANGRY, then at Flink. He raises a scolding finger at Flink, who thus is unjustly accused of having fiddled with one of the banana plugs. Once the postdoc has set ANGRY back to zero, he returns to his coffee break with Emma.

I try to call Emma, but Flink is sitting in the way, so I stop immediately. I don't like the idea of Flink playing monkey-in-the-middle and reading my billets-doux to Emma.

- Why don't you want to cooperate?! Flink asks again in his sign language. Look at me! Best treated of all Biochine's chimpanzees. Precisely because of *cooperation*.

I do not answer.

- You are just too stupid! Flink says, pulling out both his ears in order to look really dumb.

Once again I don't answer. Nor do I reply when Flink puts his black finger into the aquarium and gives me a poke. I just bow meekly. In no time at all, Flink grabs hold of the electric cable and swings himself over to the apparatus. For a moment my world is filled with stars and whirling suns. The cord stops swinging and the visual impressions resume their accustomed positions: the emergency shower to the left, the dog straight ahead, and daylight from the right. Now Flink perches atop CLEVER and zealously presses its buttons in various sequences. Figures flutter by on the screen as in a hastily flipped-through primer. At the picture of the ape with the half-peeled banana, he stops, beats his breast, scratches at the picture, and repeats time after time:

- Ape, ape, ape . . .

- Idiot, I think, which for a moment leaves him speechless.

I immediately regret my frankness. I really don't know how Flink reacts when provoked. It would be but a moment's work for him to grab some heavy object, a stand or a microscope, and throw it at the aquarium.

Instead Flink does something entirely different; he begins to tamper with the container of joy-juice, which is connected to CLEVER, and which dispenses fluid when one gives a correct answer. I scream to stop him . . . The next moment a cloud of spray covers my crown. Soon I'm soaring, climbing like a balloon filled with laughing gas up above my surroundings. The institute, the chimpanzee, Emma and the postdoctoral student vanish beneath me. My brain expands like an H-bomb's mushroom cloud, spreading itself out over gigantic fairytale realms.

14

At night the dog and I trade experiences. In the exchange I come off worse. What have I got to trade? The dog was born here. He goes on and on about the two happy periods in his life: his puppyhood and his time in the recreational park. He had six siblings. He never met his mother. He loves his time as a puppy most. They always slept in a clump, wrapped up in one another. More than once, when he ended up at the bottom, he almost suffocated. He chuckles contentedly. He does not look at me when he tells his stories. Instead he stares straight out; delivering a mental monologue with no definite address.

The other big event in his life was the recreational park. The park was large, at least twice the size of our present laboratory. In the park was a trap, of the kind used for hurling clay pigeons in the air. But this machine was loaded with sticks and balls. Not a person was present. The trap's loading and launching were controlled electronically. The machine never tired as a person does. One Easter they forgot to turn it off. For the next seven days it operated continuously. An orgy of fetching.

He becomes quiet and chews his teeth. They seem to give him trouble - he certainly doesn't need them. He gives a laugh at something I can't manage to decipher. Then he falls limp in his harness. I don't know if he's sleeping. He picks himself up out of his lethargy and starts to talk about how the rounds have been conducted over the years. For three hours we exchange observations on how procedures have changed. He thinks they go by too quickly nowadays. In the past a great deal was done by hand; they had to stop for a long time whether they wanted to or not. Now they scarcely need to take their hands out of their pockets.

I do not know how I shall pay him back in kind for his memories. In any event, I can make some up. I tell him I've received a letter from my mother. She will come for a visit. It will be so much fun. But I'm a little afraid that I've changed too much. One can scarcely expect that she'll recognize me. I don't want to see her sad. Or embarrassed.

I notice that the dog is not listening. He has no need whatsoever for my life. I allow my transferred thoughts to revolve around my mother. With the other half of my brain I think: if the dog, to all intents and purposes, has no teeth, he cannot harm me. With his long-winded old man's throat he should be able to swallow me whole. It may be tiresome and take a considerable time. But it can't be worse than being born. If I just get down into the dog's stomach, things will take care of themselves. After all these years of being drained, his stomach can have hardly any corrosive juices and enzymes left. He must be as parched and hacked to bits as a rubber tree that's been milked dry. I can continue to live in the dog's stomach. With a little luck I'll be able to push my single eye through one of its fistulae. Then it's only a matter of how we'll set the dog free. Experimental animals that have served their time are sometimes allowed to live. Maybe we'll succeed in arranging for the dog to trot along at the heels of the clerk in charge of the mail. And one day on the way back from the post office, one morning when the clerk's hands are full of parcels marked fragile - boxes of test tubes, packets containing microscope slides - one day when the clerk is standing on the same old spot without being able to decide whether to drop the important mail, or to let the poor, old, research-broken mongrel run away, then we will make a break for it! It will be no easy task to capture a dog with a human brain.

15

The day before yesterday I was in thermoradiography. It is the only trip I have made so far. I remember nothing of the journey itself because they turned off my electricity. They reconnected me in the examination room. It wasn't much to look at. The room had no windows, the lights were dimmed. They placed me in a rotating drum which scanned the heat in my various parts. If I use my sense of hearing, for example, the temperature of my temporal lobes rises - which can be recorded by thermoradiography. The psychiatrist was also present. While I was being radiographed, she showed me a number of pictures: idyllic landscapes, tasty dishes, naked women, people being tortured, and purely abstract compositions of squares and triangles. Am I healthy?

About twenty-four hours later, some big changes were made in my immediate environment. Large green sheets were laid over ANGRY, SATISFIED, LONGING, and CLEVER. Now an alpine landscape with steep slopes towers up directly opposite me. At any moment one expects a model train to come clattering out of the mouth of some tunnel. But they haven't given me a model railroad; otherwise this would be a suitable way to pass the time. Instead, they have given me a colour TV. It stands atop ANGRY, thus a little too high up for real comfort. When I lie watching TV, now and then my ear-fins have to make a few strokes so that I can find the right angle.

Both yesterday and today I've been watching children's programmes. They are very imaginative and lively. These are not real people shown on the screen but flexible cloth puppets. They are made from particoloured stockings that are slipped over the hand and arm. They portray a frog, a rooster, a pig, etc. The animals are playing, banging one another on the head with large letters made of cellulose plastic. The idea is that I learn how to spell. But since I can spell already, I prefer to lie here thinking of Emma. If they take Emma away from me, I'll have nothing left to live for.

I lie and stare at these ludicrous puppets. One of them is a monster who loves baked goods. Right now he is swallowing the microphone in the belief that it's some sort of cookie. Deep inside me I hope he will eat up the whole television set. I stare straight into the Cookie Monster's forehead to convey my will. It doesn't work at all. Why should it - the programme has been pre-recorded.

The day before yesterday, between two examinations, I discovered a new power within myself: I can influence the movements of other people, not just those of dogs. For a long time, I have been bothered occasionally by sensations from the amputated parts of my body: my back itches, a leg jumps, my stomach growls. While I was lying there, cooling off between the two tests, my left arm suddenly began to jerk. I ignored it. But at the same time I remarked how one of the technicians had trouble with his left arm: he stood and stared at his arm as it bent and his fingers spread out. That was *exactly* how I felt myself. Instantly my phantom sensations disappeared - and the technician went back to work. A while later a foreign cleaning man was in the room, a short, slender man with blue-black hair. He suddenly began to limp *at the same time as* I was feeling one of my legs fall asleep and become extremely stiff. That could not have been a coincidence. But I'm still not entirely clear as to who influenced whom; if it was I who triggered the cleaner's lameness, or if it was he who made my leg fall asleep.

16

Sunday. I lie and as usual stare at my disheartening output. On the apparatus right across from me they have taped up my speech strips; I mean what I dictated last week with the help of CLEVER's printer. The strips read: $GHHJQ_{700}P$, $MNBVCXZ$, $HGH68YT$, $QWERTYUI_9$, and $SDFTIJLK$. CLEVER has not blinked green even once; all of my utterances get a grade of fail.

On Sundays we have special routines. The research team comes only when necessary. But our needs are provided for as usual. The animals and I must have food. Indeed, there's been talk, so Emma says, of automation. Nowadays there are microcomputerized robots, which can dispense predetermined rations exactly on time. But the laboratory has not been allotted adequate funding for such a capital investment. Thus, we are cared for by more- or less-skilled assistants, who often come from different firms. Of course, errors do occur. Last Sunday they forgot all about my B-vitamins.

I have begun to map out my existence. I believe this is imperative for my survival. I use the weekends to try to gain supremacy over the rest of creation; for me this means first and foremost the dog, since the rats have been moved to the utility room. After breakfast, when we're both digesting our food, I direct my attention to the dog. I try to focus on a point directly in front of his ear. From my point of view, he's always suspended in profile. Maybe that's what's wrong. When I address myself to Emma, I aim straight at her forehead. But, as things stand, I have to try to influence the dog in profile, and that doesn't work particularly well. Now and then I have made him start to move a paw. But that could be mere coincidence.

Today isn't just any Sunday: Emma is on duty! And there's no one to disturb us. Of course the rats will get their share of her time. But there's no research team, no silly spelling exercises, no taking of specimens; they have begun to take EEGs of me almost daily. I assume it has something to do with my wretched spelling results. At first I saw this as a threat. That this could be the first indication of their intention to cashier me. But actually this is quite reassuring. The electroencephalograms show that my mind has greater vitality and quicker wits than ever. Thus, my word blindness cannot be attributed to brain damage.

Now Emma returns from weighing. The guinea pigs in the attic have to be weighed every weekend. It seems they are a part of some acoustical experiment. If they are exposed to continuous noise, their growth is arrested. Emma doesn't know very much about it, but there are some things one can figure out oneself. When Emma comes, she sees to the dog first. It doesn't make me particularly jealous because I know that she'll come to me afterwards.

The dog is let out of his harness for a while - the first time since I've come here. Emma begins to detach the tubes at their connectors and puts wads in the short tube-stumps under the dog's belly. A dozen tube-nipples hang down - giving the dog a ceremonious appearance. When he raises his nose and gazes out over the laboratory, he looks like the legendary she-wolf of Rome, the one who gave suck to Romulus and Remus.

Now Emma comes in my direction with the dog stumbling along at her heels, his legs wide apart. There is something eerie about the warm devotion of experimental animals; they never cease loving their tormentors. Emma makes instant coffee, gets herself a stool, and sits down. She leans her chin against her elbows and looks at me, as if she were sitting and staring out of a window.

- What is the dog's name? I ask.
- First you have to answer a question!
- That depends . . .
- Ypsilon, why won't you cooperate!

- But it's time you answered me a different question.
- What is it?
- Who got the tea-cosy you were knitting?
- That was a cap.
- But who was it for?

Now our positions are deadlocked. She ponders. I stare straight into her brow. Because I can convey my thoughts to her - who's to say I shouldn't also be able to *read her thoughts*, precisely like the dog's? That would give me a unique power advantage. But it's not power that I want, I want love. If I don't get love, I want power. If one cannot love, at least one can hate.

- If you aren't nice I won't read aloud for you, she says.

Now it's Emma who has the upper hand. I do so want her to read a bit for me. The information flow here in the aquarium is not quite what it ought to be. But I can't really tell the whole truth concerning my bad reading and spelling results. She can give me away - even without meaning to. I try out a half-truth:

- Because I don't want to! I say. You can't learn something you don't want to!

She looks like an unhappy bulldog and nods resignedly. I see at once that she has an understanding of the situation and that she intends to content herself with the half-answer.

- Okay, Ypsilon. I'll read to you then. But I have *no* intention of telling you whom the cap was for!

Serves me right. When she takes out the mail-order catalogue, the dog settles down, planting his chin on her knee. Naturally I'd prefer that we were alone. But of course the dog has as great a need as I for a somewhat broader outlook on life.

Emma reads from the mail-order catalogue:

- 'Otter' fibreglass canoe. Strong, roomy, and graceful. The low-profile design of bow and stern cuts wind-drift. Extra-large decks and reinforced keels. Built-in flotation chambers fore and aft make the 'Otter' unsinkable. Two watertight compartments provide plenty of room for your camera equipment and those other important items you want to keep 100% safe from water damage . . .

The dog and I nod. The dog hangs devoutly on her lips with his cow-eyes. Certainly he would prefer to hear about synthetic dog-bones and freeze-dried fish-snacks. But that's something I'd pay any price to prevent:

- Aren't they having any sales this year? I transmit.
- Final clearance! We need to make space for all our new lines, so we're clearing out our warehouse, selling things at rock bottom prices. XC Competition Class: GL4301 Fischer Europa racing skis. Fibreglass with poplar cores. Micropore finish. Sale price . . .
- Isn't there anything for an old outdoorsman?
- Anoraks. To enjoy the great outdoors means, among other things, to be properly dressed - to keep warm and dry while limiting perspiration to the minimum. Simple, functional - the classic 'pull-over' garment for hiking in the worst of weather or just for leisure wear - the anorak.
- How much are they?
- *'Fjellsikker'*, Norwegian anorak from the famed manufacturing firm UDIS. £29.95.
- Can you send away for it for me??
- You haven't got any money, Ypsilon! Do you expect me to swipe £29.95 from the coffee fund?

The dog is tired now and needs to be replaced in his suspension harness. Emma sets aside the mail-order catalogue for now. Before they go off, I ask her sternly:

- Who got the cap, Emma?!

17

The dog has been gone now for several days. They have also taken down the cradle in which he hung. The tubes have vanished. Gone, too, is the big turntable, once underneath them, which clicked empty flasks for his gastric juice into position. I imagine that the dog has served his time. That he trots along at the clerk's heels. Or maybe he trips along behind some office assistant on his way to buy Danish pastries to go with the coffee. I become a little upset at the thought of a new dog. One who is younger, sharp-toothed, impatient, and with no memories to tell me. Now that the old dog is gone, I have already forgiven him his denture-sucking, blankly-gnawing, all-consuming self-love.

This evening the dog came back! I lay sunken in my theories concerning the creation of the world. I was not cognizant of the dog's return until Emma rapped adieu on the glass. He no longer hangs in the cradle. Instead, he stands on the floor. You can see only his head and forelegs. He stands stock still. He must miss his cradle, at first a straitjacket - but with the years as dear to him as an old friend.

At once I test out my powers. Move your paw! I spark away, energetically as a newly-qualified telegraphist. But the dog does not move. Prick up an ear! Look this way! Not a single sign of life. I redouble my efforts. If I can just get the dog to move a few millimetres, over the course of months I can make further progress. Some time in the future, the dog can be my obedient servant. I can realize my plans for escape. As soon as possible I'll try to persuade Emma to send away for the canoe.

Morning comes. Emma walks in. She's all giggly and rushed. Again and again I try to have a word with her. She has no time. She's careless with my food. I get a double portion of nutrients and too little zinc. She fusses with the dog. Just before the research team arrives, she lays a sheet over him. Then she puts on her lipstick and giggles. There's something different about the research team's conduct too. The professor sports a carnation in his lapel. They position themselves in front of the dog. The post-doctoral student wriggles as if he needed to pee. Suddenly he snaps the sheet from the dog. The professor laughs. Then he lifts up the dog and embraces it. But the dog does not react. It is as rigid as a doll.

- Emma! Emma!

She tears herself away from the research team, which is marching out, and kisses the glass of my tank.

- What's happened to the dog?!

- Now don't be sad, Ypsilon. The dog was old and tired. The boss turns 60 today. We couldn't think up a better present than stuffing it. You know, they've worked together for fourteen years!

18

I am out on my second journey. Two grunting attendants have placed my aquarium on the psychiatrist's desk. First they put me - force of habit I guess - on her leather couch. As soon as she walked into the room, she gave orders to put me on the desk. Now she's sitting with a book for the deaf-and-dumb on her knees and is trying to make herself understood in sign language.

- *How are you?* she signs.

What shall I answer? I have no limbs to sign with. Had she chosen the Morse code, I could have waved my earflaps to designate dots or dashes. When I talked to the chimpanzee, I answered straight into his forehead. But I don't want to do that now. It may be wise to keep that skill to myself for a while longer.

- *You seem depressed . . .*

Quite right. After all, they have taken my roommate the dog away from me. What's worse: I recall that this is not the first time someone has been taken from me. I am extremely suspicious of my recollections. I know that they have demagnetized my memory, but now I have images in an interior darkroom - images that *must* be recollections. Why else should they upset me so? I remember lying in a bed. No, it is not an ordinary bed, it is a respirator. I am completely at the mercy of the machine's rhythm. I try to relax and let the respirator breathe for me, but all the while there's a buzzing in my skull: what if a fuse blows!

Now I remember: a woman sits next to the respirator. It is the same woman who now sits with the sign-language book on her lap, her fingers fumbling. But when she sat beside the respirator she did not fumble; she spoke right into my ear. We had seen each other several times. She knew all about my life. She was very eager. One evening she came with a proposal, I remember every single word: *We can liberate you from your body,* she said. I wanted to answer yes immediately, but she stopped me. She wanted me to think the situation over carefully. I believe we had ten conversations before she accepted my affirmative.

- *Are you being plagued by bad memories,* she manages to sign after several attempts; if Flink had been here as an interpreter, we would have been able to converse considerably more fluently.

Now I do not want to remember more. I absolutely do not want to remember how and why I ended up in a respirator. I allowed them to extract me, that is to say my brain, from my useless body and place me in an aquarium. I know that I ought to be grateful.

- *Give me a sign . . .* she implores.

But my head-mass shakes in a frenzy. My ear-fins stroke out of sync, causing me to oscillate to and fro. The shaking only increases - I cannot put a stop to it. The water churns. Finally she thrusts her ungloved hands down into the tank in order to stop me.

Then she leaves the room. I lie and stare at the streaming pools of water which spread out over the desk pad, seep into the calendar, and then branch out to engulf the pencil holder.

By the time she returns with the professor, I am completely calm. He looks at me through a magnifying glass, which hangs from a black cord around his neck. With bated breath I follow his movements. While speaking, he turns his profile toward me, so that I can read only the right halves of his lips. Nonetheless, I know the prescription: new electrical treatments.

I squeeze a little more out of my last memory: the woman in black enters. The psychiatrist stands up to greet her. Then the psychiatrist quickly leaves the room while the woman in black sits down on the edge of the bed. She touches my face without my being able to feel her touch.

19

This can't be the department for electrical shock treatment. I find myself inside an enormous, rotating, metal sphere. The inside is highly polished steel. Thin, red lines section off the globe in degrees of longitude and latitude. I can see my own reflection floating among the squares. I am no longer resting in water - but in air, in a state of complete weightlessness. The sphere is a space centrifuge.

In the mirror I see that they've hung a pair of magnets on me, like small earphones. Their function must be to repel me from the steel wall, for when the sphere rotates it acquires a charge. When it turns at high speed, the red lines - which are not painted on the interior wall but form a cage within the orb - are motionless.

In the mirror my cerebral nerves stand on end like a sprawling halo. I bear a remote resemblance to an icon, God's triangular eye surrounded by golden rays. Hovering weightless gives me a strong feeling of bliss. I feel omnipotent. Like an airplane, I perform a slow inside loop; deep inside the brain's hollows, in my innermost water-levels, I feel every change of position. Then I place myself at the focus of the sphere. This is how it must have been when the world was created: a void rotating rapidly around a golden bundle of energy.

If I were able to speak, I would allow letters and words to stream through my lips. They'd arrange themselves around me in planetary orbits, and we could blow up the centrifuge and expand through the yet-unfilled Universe. I no longer need a body or a brain. I float free. Mostly I hold myself together like a swarm of bees defending their queen. I have concentrated myself to the nucleus of a single cell. I have opened my thoughts like an umbrella to dry between the heavenly bodies and rolled myself out to a thin scroll, no thicker than the rice paper in a carrier pigeon's canister. Tonight I will enter a library, penetrate book jackets and covers and lay myself down between the pages. There I'll rest, like a handful of iron filings scattered between the lines. Tomorrow I will tell myself forth, spinning inside a tape recorder or a spider's web. I can live in the air, but I prefer to live in water. I feel more at home in fluid than in the vaporous water-colour gas that suffuses the galaxies.

I do not want to be considered something completed, something absolute. I prefer to be a suggestion, a rash word buzzing in the air; a black, freeze-dried thought-powder, or the infinitely fine, white dust that settles after a distant detonation.

But I do remain, I am captive in the gleaming sphere that spins more and more slowly, like a carousel after the gong has sounded. Gravity still has the power to come back and assert itself: I sink towards the bottom. Before I hit, they fish me up. The operator whispers into my ear:

- You will remember nothing of this after shock treatment.

20

Tonight is the Christmas party. Emma did not go home after work. All through the afternoon and the early evening hours, quite a few known and unknown persons loitered in, or in the vicinity of, the laboratory. Just a moment ago Emma locked herself in here and changed her clothes. Sheer bliss for yours truly! A gentleman without eyelids cannot, with the best will in the world, close his eyes.

Now they are sitting somewhere, eating. When I use my full powers of concentration, from clear out of the blue I can discern chewings, throat contractions, peristalsis, and various nerve signals to diverse organs of digestion. The field telephones are overheating. My own intestine begins to twitch a little too. Emma has told me about the Christmas presents. Not in detail but in principle. She refuses to reveal to me who will get the knitted cap.

The dancing has begun and Emma has made her way into the laboratory because she has to vomit. She sits on a stool, leans backward, and props her elbows up on the lab bench behind her. Her head is thrown back, the neck of her dress is unbuttoned, and her mouth is wide open. She forces herself to puff and blow, as during labour. Now and then she breaks off and gets about halfway up from the stool, but then she resumes her laboured breathing. Sweat breaks out on her forehead. Now she gets up precipitously, and with her hand covering her mouth, she gets down on her knees near the drain for the emergency shower. Powerless to help her, I tear at my moorings - I so want to get up and lay a cool hand on her forehead.

Instead the postdoctoral student comes in. He is still wearing the cap from his Santa outfit, after having distributed the presents. In one of his hands he has a cup of glögg, in the other a bunch of gingersnaps. When he catches sight of me, he tosses his head jauntily and comes forward. He gives me a meaningful wink and leans a gingersnap pig against the aquarium. I hang on his lips to get my 'Merry Christmas'. But he says nothing, he just grins significantly, as if at some feeble-minded person. After he notices Emma kneeling by the shower, he discreetly leaves the premises.

Thirty minutes vanish, let loose one after another like confetti in the wind. By degrees, Emma raises herself up from her degradation: spits, lets the water run, gargles, washes herself, combs her hair, buttons her dress, paints her lips, and plucks away the false eyelashes that have come loose at the corners. She comes and sits with me. Very soon her forehead sinks down in the bend of her arm. Her head shifts to a comfortable position and she falls asleep in an adoring pose - as if she were worshipping the gingersnap pig propped up against the aquarium. I leave her to her dreamless sleep for a while. Then I go into her blacked-out skull and illuminate it with promises of gold and soft fabrics. But I go at it a little too forcefully: she wakes up with a start and looks vacantly first at the pig and then at me. Has the pig forced his way between us with indecent suggestions?

The postdoc comes back with a mug of coffee in each hand. He sits down very close to Emma. They divide the pig between them. The postdoc quickly eats his piece, while Emma carelessly dunks the pig's rump until it vanishes in the coffee.

- Feeling . . . better . . .? the postdoc asks, talking with crumbs in the corners of his mouth.

- Only had half a glass of glögg, Emma says.

They remain sitting in silence with their heads in their hands like an old, tired, married couple at a bar. The chronometer on the bench behind them nags on: 23.01.44, 23.01.45, 23.01.46 . . . If I had the physical capability, I would get rid of the man and pull the woman back to me back here behind the counter. There is so much I would like to confide to her.

Now the psychiatrist comes back to fetch the postdoc. She pushes in between him and Emma with a branch of mistletoe and waves it over their heads. When she does not succeed in getting them to kiss, she drags the postdoc away to the dance.

Alone at last.

- Emma, there is something I would like to tell you . . .

She nods sleepily, then pulls herself together and gulps down the cold coffee. And makes a wry face at the disintegrating gingersnap.

- It's about the reading exercises, I convey to her forehead.
- I'm not hearing quite right, she mouths.
- The reading exercises. This elementary school the researchers are trying to force me to enrol in.
- You mean CLEVER?
- Precisely. All this crap about showing me a picture of an ape and then getting me to say the letter A in Morse code.
- What about it?
- You've already asked me the question several times: why I will not cooperate.
- Can you read, then?
- Of course I can. If the researchers are going to lay millions on the line to keep a human brain alive in an aquarium, they sure as hell aren't going to choose an illiterate.
- That's worth thinking about.
- Right you are.
- Go on, then, Ypsilon, she mouths sleepily.
- Well, it's like this: if I answer correctly, if I signal the letter A when they show me the ape, do you know what happens then? Then I get a squirt of joy-juice from the container that sits on CLEVER.
- And?
- And do you know how that makes you feel?
- High.
- Exactly.
- But don't you want to feel high?

- Oh, yes. I mean no. I do not want to develop a dependency, you understand. I do not want to get addicted to that joy-juice. I don't want to lie here longing for it; I do not want to get high on their terms, can't you see?

- But surely it is non-addictive. The professor is very careful about such things.

- Of course, but don't you see! One fine day they won't even need the joy-juice! One fine day I will have become so conditioned that all they will have to do is show me the ape and I'll have the letter A on my tongue . . . and I'll feel high entirely of my own accord!

- Wow, that's fantastic!

- Not at all fantastic. I feel I'm being duped, don't you see?

- I wonder if you're not just a little ungrateful all the same . . .

- No, Emma! You have to understand. You are the only person I have faith in. You must grasp this! They can start manipulating me however the hell they please. They can trot out another image, some ingenious mathematical brainteaser, something I'll never be able to solve. And each time I get it wrong, they can squirt me with something that induces anxiety or that makes me shit all over myself! I don't want to be a slave to chemicals!

- But aren't we all, though . . . when it comes down to it?

Clearly she is right. From a materialistic view of the human condition, the life of the soul is nothing but physics and chemistry. But still she is wrong: in practice the finer mechanisms are hidden from us, allowing us to experience ourselves as reasonably free and independent individuals.

- Don't be sad, Ypsilon. To me you are no machine! To me you are . . .

- What?

- Just like any other human being!

- Am I?

- At the very least. Actually you're also my buddy.

- Nothing more?

- Don't be silly now.

We look deep into each other's eyes for a while, then she starts to grin. I like her best when she's happy.

- You know what, Ypsilon?
- No, what?
- It's a pity it's not time for your bath. I would like to bathe you, and then I would put you in a towel and hold you in my lap a long time. And then dry you off very, very carefully.

21

I lie watching a film. The room is in half darkness. A projection screen is set up in the pathway between the lab benches. The film is in colour, but badly spliced, glaring, and grainy. I am not alone in the room. To my left sits a young man in an unbuttoned white coat. Next to him on the bench sits a chimpanzee in a white coat that is buttoned up to his throat. We are watching the film together.

The film shows some sort of scientific experiment. By way of introduction, the camera pans over a laboratory with diverse pieces of electronic equipment. The camera focuses on a hood. Inside it is an oblong glass tank filled with water. From inside the top of the hood, long tangled skeins of thin electrical cords feed down into the glass tank. A man in a white coat - it is the same young man who is sitting beside me - fiddles with the cords. The film suddenly leaps forward in time: the man is standing with a towel over his hands. In the towel rests a yellowish-pink blob, which he holds forward for the camera. It is impossible to identify the object. It bears a remote resemblance to a kilo of ground pork packed in plastic.

New scene: a small, cramped room. In the middle of the room stands a plank bed with a rubber-coated mattress. The bed is narrow and has constraints for the hands and feet. At the head of the bed stands a yellow sheet-metal box on high legs that have casters. The box has a couple of round dials on top. Hanging on a hook is something that looks like a pair of heavy-duty, black headphones. The man with the towel is suddenly standing at the head of the bed. He places the yellowish-red blob down on it. Then he takes a plastic bottle with a spray-nozzle, the kind one uses when ironing shirts, and sprinkles watery fluid over the blob. Another man in a white coat stands near the yellow sheet-metal box. He seems nervous and tense. He holds the black, heavy-duty headphones in his hands. A chimpanzee standing on his toes beside a round, steel stool can be glimpsed in the background.

The nervous man puts the headphones on the blob. One red and one black cord lead from the phones to the sheet-metal box. An older man comes into the room. He is calm and friendly. He greets the two others, ruffles the chimp's hair, and bends over the blob with its headphones, checking to see that all is fastened correctly. He gives the blob a little pat.

Close-up of the yellow sheet-metal box. On the box is a switch that can be turned to an 'on' or an 'off' position. The hand of the calm man turns the black switch from 'off' to 'on'. Close-up of the blob with headphones. The surface of the blob alternately jerks and billows out in slow wave-beats. The procedure is repeated three times. An ammeter can also be seen in the frame; its needle jumps quickly to the right, only to toil back tiredly afterwards to its starting position. In the final shot, the younger man, now at the head of the bed, smiles and makes the V sign.

The film is over. The lights are turned on. The screen is put away. The projector, which stood right beside me, is packed into a white styrofoam box. Everyone but the older, calm, and likeable man leaves the room. He stands right in front of me, holding the chimpanzee's hand. While chewing on a carrot, the chimp looks up affectionately into the man's face.

The man leans close to me, moving his lips slowly and in an exaggerated fashion. I try to follow. It's slow going. I know that he's trying to tell me something, but I can't quite make it out. Instead the man takes the chimp up in his arms. With the carrot now plugged in one corner of his mouth like a cigar, the chimp signs to me with his hands. I try to interpret the signs. I really do know what the signs stand for, but I have a hard time putting them together into words; like a long-pensioned naval officer trying to read a message in semaphore. Suddenly the man puts the chimp down on the floor and begins to scold him with a raised index finger. He sits there sulking. The man bends down over me again and grimaces with his lips. I believe he is saying:

- Do you know me?

I recognize the face. But I can't really place it. He repeats the question and I want to answer, but I don't really know how. My ears make a couple of strokes - I didn't know I could wiggle my ears - and in this way I nod an affirmation.

The man nods back at me, bends closer, and says:

- I am the one called the professor. But actually my name is George.

I nod and curtsey and try to install the name in my memory. When I try to remember it hurts inside me. My whole skull feels incredibly dizzy, as if I had run smack into a wall.

- You'll feel better tomorrow, says the man whose name is George.

A young woman comes forward and smiles at me. She has a thin nose and a bloated mouth. She leans down over me and says:

- Hi, it's me Emma. Though you don't remember me just now. After the shock treatment.

Emma and George, I determine to place these names in my memory. I would also like to put a few questions to these two. But I don't manage to figure out how to do this. One moment it feels as if I had a mouth, the next it seems my mouth has been blown away. Nothing but tepid water laps my gums.

George - was that his name? - says something again. I don't understand at first and he must repeat it:

- Clever, he says and pecks encouragingly at the aquarium with his finger.

I put this in my memory. Because his name is George and the lady's name is . . . Mamma?, then my name, by process of elimination, must be Clever. The young woman lowers a micro-pipette into my tank and sucks up a little fluid.

- His IQ is down below 200 now, she says to George.

To hell with their system of values. Instead of bothering myself

71

about it, I try to learn my name by heart: My name is 'Clever', I tell myself over and over again.

22

I don't think we ever learn how we look. Every picture of us appears as a misrepresentation. They have now shown the film of my undergoing electrical shock treatment four times. After each of the last three screenings, George said:

- You must accept that that is *you*.

I would so like to accept. But at the same time I don't want to be dishonest. I cannot get it into my head that that greyish-pink, furrowed blob in the film is supposed to be me. It's such a comedown.

- Look at me, George says, rolling up his sleeves and unbuttoning the top of his shirt so that his chest can be seen. What *real* difference is there?

We converse using an apparatus that stands next to me but at an angle of 90 degrees, so that I can constantly scan it out of the corner of my eye. This device has a picture tube. On the screen is a pair of lips. When I think the word 'hi', the lips form, with ridiculously exaggerated clarity, 'HHHHHHIIIIIII'. I can talk to myself if I want to. When I get up in the morning I can say, 'Hello to you, you old galosh!' 'Galosh' is one of the practice words. They've urged me to practise whenever I have a free moment. I am already more proficient than George at forming 'galosh' - but of course the comparison is a bit unfair: I have the benefit of the latest in electronics, while George only has recourse to his ordinary, old pair of lips.

One of our problems is that George is always having to turn his head. When he speaks to me, he must keep his mouth right in front of me. I need to see both corners of his mouth. But when I speak, George has to turn his head to the side. Otherwise he can't see the screen. I have proposed that they get two screens, a large one for the bench in front of me, from which I could read off my own speech - plus a little one that would stand beside me and from which the personnel could read without having to take their eyes off me. But it's too expensive.

- But a mirror can't cost so very much?

Now they are trying to dig up a mirror. The lady whose name is not Mamma but Emma has gone to look for one. Meanwhile, George keeps up his nagging:

- If I showed you your heart and said: This is you. Would you deny it then?

How does one answer such a question? Here they are capable of laying out a huge spread of whatever they want: heart, kidneys, liver, lungs. How would I be able to recognize myself?

- You are prejudiced, Clever, George replies. Why get hung up on a face? Let us suppose that every human being went around with his heart, a reddish-brown, pulsating mass, on top of his neck. We would soon see that our hearts are not all identical. Just like the Chinese, Clever. Anyone who has been to China no longer believes that all Chinese look alike.

- Have you been to China?

When he turns back to face me after having read off this question, he is visibly displeased.

- How do you really feel, Clever? I'm beginning to wonder if we haven't given you a few too many shocks? You're functioning way below your own level. Do you really feel like you're lying at an IQ level of around 300?

- Honestly speaking, no.

- But don't you feel like you're making progress?

- A fingersbreadth a day, sometimes two.

George has some trouble reading off 'fingersbreadth' on the lip-screen; he's not really a skilled lipreader.

- *Millimetre!* I alter my reply.

Now Emma returns with the mirror. I'm a little standoffish

towards Emma; she seems at once so near and yet so far away. Did we go to school together? When I get a chance to I'll ask her. Emma is more at home in lip-language than George is. She places the mirror in front of me; George says:

- Take a good look now, Clever. That is *you.*

I take a good look. Close up, maybe I don't look as dumb as in the film. There's a distinct sparkle in my eye. My ears are well-formed, even if they stick out a bit. I don't look as utterly defenceless lying here in the aquarium as I do in the film, when I was being carried around in a moistened towel.

- That does seem to be me, I say somewhat halfheartedly.

Then we try to use the mirror in place of a second picture screen. But it does not work out: whether we place the mirror on the bench and the screen beside me, or vice versa, the mirror-image is too small. But the most disorienting thing is the reversed perspective in the mirror, that left becomes right and right becomes left. Now, one would think that this would not make any difference; but mouths are no different from the two halves of the face, one half stands in a dialectical relationship to the other. Presumably the same is true of the brain's two hemispheres: one of them houses feeling, the other intellect. A spiritual life can flourish only in a fertile state of opposition between right and left.

Soon I will be operated on and have a silver wire implanted in me. The wire will run from my speech centre to a short antenna high up on top of my brain. Through the antenna I will be able to transmit my speech directly to my surroundings. The only equipment they, on their side, will need is an ordinary pair of hearing-aid eyeglasses.

When Emma takes the mirror away, she says:

- Too bad that the mirror didn't work, Ypsilon.

- My name is Clever and not Ypsilon!

- George laughs and looks at Emma:

- No, 'Clever'. You've got it reversed. Your name is Ypsilon. Once all the pieces fall back into place, you'll realize that.

For the first few days after they'd blasted my memory with

electrical shocks, I felt nothing but euphoria and bliss; as if I were hovering half a metre above the earth's surface, liberated from the whole rubbish pile of old recollections. Now, that feeling is beginning to subside. Instead, I am treading water and trying to get a foothold, to reach a stone or some other solid object. When Emma said Ypsilon, for a moment it felt as if I had found one. But almost immediately I slipped off it again, as if the name Ypsilon had been smeared with soap. Is that really my original name? Emma? Emma! Bend down and kiss me. No, I'm not asking, like the frog, to be turned back into a prince. Just give me a body.

23

When the ape drags a chair forward and climbs up on it, I get
scared. He's wearing a round, knitted cap that looks like the beret
on an acorn. The ape signs and grimaces. It is the same chimpanzee George had with him the other day. He makes me feel ill at
ease. First I don't bother to read what the ape is signing. But I
can hardly turn away. I would like to turn away. When a dimwit
forces himself upon you, spitting and hissing in your face,
instinctively you turn your profile toward him.

But the ape does not relent. All the more slowly and distinctly
he signs:

- My name is Flink. My name is Flink . . .

The name says nothing to me. But to calm down the ape, I
switch on my thought transference.

- And mine is Clever.

The ape doesn't like this. First he stares in astonishment, then
he bursts into a cascade of gestures - as when one has brutally
awakened someone from a deep sleep.

- Your name is Y-p-s-i-l-o-n.

- My name is Clever, I reply. You are mistaken.

The ape lowers his long crane-arms, lays his head with its
knitted cap to one side, and looks very distressed.

- You will remember, he signs.

I don't want to remember. I want to start afresh. As soon as I
try to remember, I get a migraine. I feel best when I try to stare
straight ahead, never glancing to either side or over my shoulder.

- We must help each other to remember, says the ape.

I know nothing about the ape. He usually accompanies George. That is all I know. How then could I assume any responsibility whatsoever for the ape's past.

- We will make an agreement, says the ape. We will preserve our memories in each other. If you will tell me your life story, I will study it till I have it by heart. Then if they later set you back to zero with electricity, I'll tell it to you afterwards.

- And I? You must want something in exchange?

- That you will do the same for me.

- There's nothing to tell. I know nothing about you. I know next to nothing about myself.

- Yes you do! You always know something!

Suddenly the ape straightens up. What time is it? Time for food, the rounds, the security guard checking to see that no taps have been left running? The ape hops down, pushes the chair back to where it was. Before he goes, he rises up on tiptoe towards me and gesticulates:

- We are friends. Don't you forget it. But we must not show that we are friends. Or they won't allow us to meet.

24

Visiting the dentist is like being knocked down on to your back and raped in the mouth. Of course I don't have a mouth. They have swaddled the dental chair's headrest in towels and propped me up on it, so that I lie with my eye aimed straight up at the huge, blinding lamp. Several people crouch around me; out of the corner of my eye I can just make out George - called the professor - as well as two or three other men with masks over their mouths and with bare forearms. In the mirrors that surround the intense light bulb I can see them working. One of them holds a spray-flask, another holds a suction apparatus, a third holds a slender, pointed instrument that brings to mind a drill. Now that I'm on dry land, I can perceive distinct sounds. I hear the scraping of metal, water flushing down a drain, something that hisses, someone scraping one of his feet on the floor; brusque muttering behind the facemasks.

Suddenly George says:

- Lie still, Ypsilon, all we're going to do is take an X-ray.

Everyone vanishes. Alone in the chair's headrest I wait, holding my breath. It is not difficult to keep still. After all, the only movement I can accomplish is wiggling my ears. And that's something I have not dared attempt on dry land. I have lived for so long in water that I am afraid of the air, afraid of drying out, afraid that my ears or my gills or whatever they are that droop beside my temporal lobes - that in the absence of water these hunks of skin will quickly crumple up and irremediably stiffen into huge cornflakes, of no use whatsoever for any sort of swimming.

My attentiveness rises to a fevered pitch in anticipation of the X-ray. This is how it must feel to wait for an execution squad to drop down on one knee, take aim, and . . . I hear a faint 'click' from the X-ray machine. Of course I can't feel a thing. Millions of small particles penetrate my brain-tissue and I don't notice it in the least. Isn't this, if anything, proof that the soul must be located somewhere else? Maybe at this very moment it hovers over me like a big, invisible speech balloon, a thin, transparent, plastic bag with its root thrust down in one of the brain's convolutions; a genie on its way out of the bottle, but captured for analysis.

They come back into the room and automatically I open wide. But they are not interested in what once was my mouth. They are working up on top of my crown. A brain completely lacks the ability to feel pain - but when they poke around in me I can feel light tickling sensations. And my skin feels tight. I am grateful that they don't try to converse with me about the wind and the weather, films or the theatre. To lie in a dentist's chair and not to be able to answer . . . I know this happened to me before, but when? Where? Not all that many years ago, in any case. Had I been born in the nineteenth century, I would hardly feel at home amidst all this plastic and stainless steel. If that were the case, I would be expecting polished wood, cast iron, a spiral drill driven by a spinning-wheel treadle, and ornate instruments with elaborate painted designs. Men not in white but in frock coats.

- We need to take one more X-ray, George says. The last one. So we can be sure that you're wired correctly.

Again they all disappear. I concentrate on the radiation. I don't know if this is an illusion, but I believe I can feel billions of elementary particles passing through the mass of my brain; they sail through in loose clusters, slowly, majestically, and utterly silently, as in an opera in outer space.

Only now do I realize that I have heard George speak to me! I could not have read his lips, he *spoke*. A miracle?! No, there's an entirely natural explanation. The thin silver antenna that George mentioned long ago is implanted in my centre for speech and hearing. Presumably they need some additional equipment: a few printed circuits, a crystal diode . . . what do I know; the spin-off products of scientific research are far too numerous to keep up with.

- Ypsilon! Lie still now so we can fix the outgoing connection!

Devoutly I stare up into the mirror of the ceiling lamp. Eight flat mirrors surround the actual source of light. In these eight small squares the same image repeats itself: Four backs, clad in white, ankle-length coats that tie up the back, lean over me. I am the pale, wrinkled blob in the centre - not unlike a newborn, thrusting its swollen, puckered-up face into the open air. Nowadays I have accepted on an intellectual level that I am an isolated brain - but deep down in my soul, wherever that now happens to be, I am a fine figure of a man with clear-cut features and a cheerfully playful gaze.

George holds a glistening needle between his thumb and index finger. For a moment it flashes like a magician's wand. Then he sinks the needle into me.

- Now it's done. How does it feel?
- First-rate!
- Wait . . . I forgot the hearing-aid glasses.
- First-rate! I repeat.
- First-rate!! George cries out with such force that I nearly fly out of the chair.
- Turn down the volume if you're going to scream, I say.
- Fantastic, he whispers, bending down toward my eye. Fantastic, Ypsilon! If you had a mouth I would kiss it.

They all shake hands with one another - myself excepted. This is a huge scientific breakthrough. Only now that they have succeeded in establishing a technically uncomplicated two-way system of communication with me, can we really begin to work together in all seriousness. Our earlier achievements were, more or less, a series of circus acts under the high patronage of science; a documented and recorded game, as when one teaches pigeons to play pachisi with the help of conditioned reflexes.

Then everyone wants to talk with me. The hearing-aid glasses wander from one to the other. But they are so eager to speak with the software in the dentist's chair that they neglect to introduce themselves.

- Who is talking now? I have to ask all the time. Is it you who are called the Postdoctoral Student?

They cackle and monkey around as if they had already drunk the champagne, which doubtless is on ice in one of Biochine's numerous refrigerators. One after the other they now come forward and bow:

- My name is Peter. Pleased to meet you!
- And my name is Curt. Hi!

How can I know that the postdoc, that is to say Curt, spells his name with a C? No problem, I just *know*. When they speak I also hear a faint background babbling. Is this interference from the radio? No it is not: it is their thoughts. I can latch on to only a few words in the stream of their thoughts, but with a little practice I am sure I will be able to follow their thinking more or less fluently. And what do they hear? Do they hear my thoughts?! I say to Curt:

- Nice name you have. Short and easy to remember.

At the same time I think as plainly as I can: if I had an axe I would slam it right through your face and send you splattering all over the walls!

But all Curt does is smile, wave both his hands, and pout his lips happily, as if he were bending over a cradle. But I don't look like a baby. When I focus on myself in the lamp's eight mirrors I see the obligatorily pale blob with one pointy ear on either side - and now with two silver antennae sticking out from its frontal lobes. No, I don't look like a newborn; more like something that's fallen from Mars.

25

Today is Sunday. One of the extra attendants has fed me. For a long time he stood contemplating the instructions for my care, poking about among the pipettes on the meal-cart. There was no point in trying to talk to him. Someone had locked up the hearing-aid glasses for the weekend. But he did manage to feed me, even if it took three times as long as it should have. Afterwards we were both equally relieved; he opened a pilsner and I laid myself down at the bottom of the aquarium to invent something for Flink in peace and quiet. Before you know it he'll be along with his 'memory contract': if I tell you my story, you must tell me yours.

But I was not left in peace. As soon as the attendant marched off with the meal-cart, George came in, carefully closing the door behind him. In his left hand he held his ordinary, half-moon-shaped reading glasses - in his right the heavier, black-rimmed hearing-aid glasses. He pulled out a stool, settled himself down, put on the hearing-aid glasses and adjusted them painstakingly, as if he were about to listen to a violin recital.

- I'm not disturbing you, am I??

- Not at all, I reply; now that we can speak directly with each other, I feel more uncertain, more exposed - with the earlier, more complicated systems, I always had more time to think.

- The unpleasant thing about being in charge is that one cannot confide in anyone, George says. We have a fine working climate here, great team spirit; but still you have to understand, Ypsilon, that one cannot speak absolutely candidly to a subordinate. And when it comes to the management of the corporation . . . Well, let's just leave it at that. Can I rely on your discretion?

- No.
- No??
- You know best about that yourself. How can I know how classified the contents of my thoughts are? Maybe you and your co-workers can go right into me, as in a memory bank, provided you have the right data key?
- Utopias! he laughs. Nobody yet has succeeded in peering straight into a brain.
- But what about my memory? The memory I get shock treatments for?
- That's the end of that, now. We have not achieved what we had hoped.
- Namely?
- Expressed simply: freeing the storage capacity of your cortex. Stupidly enough, we believed that if we demagnetized your memory, there would be blank surfaces left over.
- As when one erases a cassette tape??
- I'll concede that the theory was a little too simple.
- So I won't get any more shocks now?
- If it were possible, I would shake your hand on that. No, we were barking up the wrong tree, so to speak . . . Of course we can at least blast away parts of your memory. But the void has an uncanny ability to fill itself in again with pseudo-memories, free fantasies. Moreover, we cannot utilize the memory-content we blast out of your brain. It vanishes into thin air, so to speak.
- But shouldn't we be talking about me??
- Since it's Sunday, we can talk about me instead . . . If you don't have anything in particular against it??
- Maybe it is about time we got to know each other?
- Exactly, Ypsilon. I just don't know where to begin. It seems so trivial, sitting here and gossiping about Biochine and this lab. Allow me instead to tell you something personal. We all have a dream, don't we?

I make no reply. I am not supposed to. There are people who

end practically every sentence with 'isn't that so?' They only get annoyed if one replies.

- Have you been to Paris?

I don't answer this one either.

- If you have been to Paris, Ypsilon, surely you have visited the Musée de l'Homme, in the Chaillot Palace, directly opposite the Eiffel Tower; I would venture to call it a Mecca for anthropology. In it there's everything from Hottentot hairdos to Polynesian canoes. But I want to recommend the unofficial wing. Assuming, of course, that one has contacts. Frenchmen, as you know, have a certain tendency to be bureaucratic. If one has a penchant for the macabre, one can browse through the collection of shrunken heads from New Guinea, or the cylindrical glass bottles containing whole heads in alcohol. During colonial times, it seems there was an almost manic passion to collect things. From all the corners of the French Empire came the heads of decapitated evil-doers, diverse curiosities, and deformities. There must have been money provided for the scientific purchases. But beyond the collection of heads in alcohol, there's something far more interesting, the phrenological section. You know, all that business about lumps and abscesses on the outside of the skull or the brain, and the relationships these bumps have to character traits. Incidentally, an approach that's making a comeback in the field of neuroanatomy. But, Ypsilon, in one particular cabinet is the world's finest collection of distinguished brains.

- In alcohol?

- Rather in formalin. Of course they don't have Einstein. His brain is said to lie in a jar under a refrigerator in Wichita. But there are others; Paul Broca, for example.

He leans forward and looks at me with an expectant expression.

- There's no point in trying to give me some kind of exam, George . . .

- It was Broca who found the centre for speech in the human brain, Ypsilon. And initiated a very fruitful project of mapping. The greatest neuroanatomist of the nineteenth century. Neurology's Newton! Now, each year we can mark off more and more narrowly delimited areas of the brain along with their functions. Not just such rudimentary functions as muscular movements . . . Memory functions, learning centres. We no longer find ourselves - as someone once said - in the era of Columbus. We no longer randomly sail around on the hemispheres of the brain. We are down to the stage of land surveyors, staking out smaller and more exact plots. And it was Broca who began all this!

- You had a dream??

- We, all of us, have a dream. My associates here would laugh or smile with embarrassment if I confided mine to them. The Nobel Prize no longer has any status; it has become a group prize. There is a narrower needle's eye: after death to be placed on the same shelf as Broca.

26

The girl who gives me food is called Emma. My skull is filled with ravenous young birds who cry out for new memories. I give them a serving of Emma. Emma's face with its thin nose and its smeary lips. Then I stuff Emma's hair into them. It is dark blonde. She almost always wears a roomy crêpe cap; I stuff the cap into my memory. I also pack in her clogs. Her hands. The rubber gloves on her hands. The green coat. The rubber apron she wears when she's cleaning. Her voice. Her gaze. Her name - Emma, letter for letter.

Emma behaves as if we have known each other for a long time. That makes me happy. I don't want to fall in love with Emma. There is something unnatural about patients falling for their nurses. Only because there is no other choice. But whom else shall I love? The ape?

All evening long I lie here, rehearsing what I would like to say to Emma. When I get her to myself, I will whisper, 'Crawl in with me!' I wish I were a sea turtle as big as a boulder. So strong that Emma could ride naked on my back without being washed away. Purely anatomically, I already bear some resemblance to a sea turtle: a rounded, humpbacked blob with a little orb up front, pendulating on its stem. With time, my ears will certainly come more and more to resemble a sea turtle's flippers. I want us to settle down somewhere in the Indian Ocean, in a lagoon of the Maldive Islands or the Seychelles. We can spend the nights in a coral cave, Emma sleeping on a rock shelf while I rest moored in the water down below. We will devote the days to diving. With her on my back, I will comb the sunken cities for Spanish ducats.

27

I have a new appointment with the psychiatrist. There's a touch of ceremony in being carried into her room for a private session; something entirely different from seeing her standing and gaping over George's shoulder when they make the morning rounds. This is the first time we can talk with each other. My silver antennae enable me to transmit directly to the hearing-aid glasses she has borrowed from George - and to receive her speech even though I'm resting below the surface of the water. Although my ears function marvellously well. Actually, I could lie on a towel in her lap and converse, but I might become too dry, especially in the eye. Thus, I remain in my aquarium. They have not put me on her desk this time, but on the low table in front of the sofa. It feels more relaxed this way.

She says:

- A Greek philosopher compared our body with a big bear that is always lumbering at our heels. A big, unfamiliar brute, very close by, yours alone and yet a complete stranger to you. Clever, do you know what I am talking about? Unlike the rest of us, you no longer have a body, a 'bear' at your heels. That must feel enormously liberating?!

Her way of immediately directing the conversation irritates me. I haven't come here to talk philosophy. *I want to know what they intend to do with me!* Will I get to keep my identity? If so, it is my right as a human being to know.

- I have come to you to talk about my future, I say. Besides, my name is Ypsilon. Not Clever.

- But wasn't it you who christened yourself 'Clever'? . . .
- What do you know about my future?
- That is George's department.
- I am asking you what *you* know.
- Not much. My area of expertise and my assignment is your spiritual life.
- What do they intend to do with me?!
- You are to have fascinating working assignments. Of that I am absolutely certain. But first we must take the opportunity to learn more about how you function. So that we can take care of you properly. For example, you wouldn't like it if we put you in too strong a solution, or if we used the wrong amperage.
- WHAT DO YOU INTEND TO DO WITH ME, I scream so loud that she tears off the hearing-aid glasses.
She massages her eyes, pulls herself together, straightens her back, and puts the glasses back on.
- You are here wholly of your own free will, isn't that so?
- That's what you say!
- We have it in writing. Witnesses. With your own signature. Where you *voluntarily* consent to let us take charge of you. You have already been given complete information about it all.
- What good does that do me when I don't know my name, when I wouldn't recognize my own signature if you stuck it right under my nose. You know I have forgotten *everything!*
- That's just the point! In order to give you a fabulous future we were obliged to wash away your past. We had to liberate your cerebral cortex from a mass of old recollections, so that you will be able to assimilate new skills.
- What new skills?!
- I am not authorized to say. George is the one in charge of the experiment. But if you ask him I don't think he'll answer you. That's part of the agreement. You are a new person now.
I give up. I make a stroke with my left ear so that my flank is towards her. Sullenly I sink towards the bottom.
- Don't sulk. I have asked you here to check on your memory. The tests indicate that we did not remove everything during your

last shock treatment.

- 'Did not remove everything.' Don't talk to me as if I had cancer! Recollections are not goddamn metastases! Besides, George has given me his word that I'm not to have any more electric shock treatments!

- Now, it's up to you to decide, she says sternly. Either we get damned furious with each other and quarrel, in which case I'll have to call up the lab and get someone to test your hormone levels . . . Or else we continue to check on your memory on amicable terms. Okay?

- Okay.

- I have with me some photographs that I want you to look at. I want to see how you react. Actually, we ought to attach the EEG-machine to you, but that feels so formal. If you promise to be completely honest, it will be enough for me to jot down what you say. Can we agree on this? Okay?

- Okay.

She sets up four photographs in a small frame in front of the aquarium. All of them portray older women, I guess they range between 60 and 75 years of age. The photos themselves are not old, but look glossy, newly taken, almost damp.

- Well, I say: Four old ladies. *So what?*

She has a writing pad on her knees and pretends to take notes. Actually, she is just sitting there tracing an endless series of squared-off meanders, in the belief that I don't see. And I don't see. But I feel the movement in her hand: monotonous, angular. Her thoughts are off elsewhere, only her hand keeps up appearances.

I make myself comfortable and wait.

- Well?

- Four old ladies, I repeat.

- Does any one of them mean anything special to you?

I look at them again. One wears glasses, the second smiles with new teeth, the third has strikingly angular and masculine features, the fourth has cheeks like shrivelled-up apples and a receding chin.

- No . . .

- One of the women is a close relative of yours.

- Tell me her name!

- There's no point in doing that. If you do not recognize her face you will not remember her name. That's how the brain operates.

- Is she still alive, the woman in the picture?

- That's something I really don't know.

- You must give me a clue . . .

- Let us keep to the rules of the game for now. Doesn't any one of the faces say something to you?

I do not reply. It's no good. I remember nothing. And that's the truth.

- I hadn't thought about giving you any clues. But think it over. I said, 'a close relative'. Who can that be?

- A mother, a daughter, a sister, a wife?

- Yes, Clever . . . Ypsilon.

- Which?

She sits quietly for two or three minutes to give me time to remember. For a moment another image flickers by: the woman in black, who comes to visit my sickbed, leads a child by the hand. But this can just as well be a fantasy.

- I cannot remember, however much I want to . . .

- Then we'll put the photos aside. Is there anything else you want to get off your chest? You can come here whenever you want to, and talk with me. Just say so during the rounds. Okay?

- Okay.

While they're carrying me back, I try to make an appraisal of the new knowledge of my past. The women in the pictures are between 60 and 75 years old. If one of them is my mother, I myself ought to be around 40. But if one of them is my daughter?

28

Emma and the postdoctoral student - whose name is actually Curt - have carried me out of the lab to the utility room. For a fleeting moment I got the idea that we were on our way to the garbage disposal. But I realized how foolish the thought was: I am worth more than my weight in gold. The reason for this temporary move also proved to be an entirely different one: the electricians needed to do some work in the laboratory. What set off my momentary fear of death? Could it have been that the water I rest in feels unstable when they lift the aquarium? I will talk to the professor. He ought to be able to account for the relationship between motion sickness and anxiety.

Now I'm standing in my water-tank on the sink between bottles and stainless steel bowls. Because the connection to the power main is makeshift, Emma stays and watches over me. She has curled up on the sink counter opposite me. Her head rests against her drawn-up knees, her left arm encircles her lower legs, her right arm acts as a fan for the smoke from her cigarette. A Christmas catalogue from a big department store lies beside her. When people read to me, they almost always read from various catalogues and prospectuses. These seem to be the only alternative to comic books. Comic books bore me to tears; and so I have to put up with the catalogues from furniture warehouses, hardware store chains, Dutch tulip cultivators, or the laconic descriptions of freeze-dried soups for mountain climbers.

Daily newspapers are strictly forbidden. The professor has given me two entirely different reasons for this: the papers are always full of the same old things, which is why they would bore me – and: nowadays the papers contain nothing but war and misery, which would upset me. If I get upset, they may be obliged to make 'neurochemical corrections', that is to say, to add tranquillizing fluids to the water in my aquarium. We have agreed that such things ought to be avoided. The milieu in which I live is already sufficiently artificial.

– How do you *really* feel? Emma asks; she doesn't bother with the hearing-aid glasses – we prefer our own system of lipreading and thought transference.

– As long as you are nearby, I fear nothing.

– Ypsilon, it's not good for you to become too attached to just one person.

– I can't help it.

The smoke rises right up into her eyes now. Coughing and blinking, she stubs out her cigarette in the drain.

– But if for some reason I could not go on working here . . . would you crack up, then?

– They won't allow me to do that.

– Please don't think me silly, but sometimes I've thought along these lines: why can't Ypsilon come home with me in the evenings and live in an aquarium in my kitchen, and then come back with me in the mornings so they can do their experiments . . .

– Have you asked them?

– Don't be absurd!

Emma lights a new cigarette, snatches up the Christmas catalogue and says:

– Shall I read to you about Toyland?

– I know you've got something else on your mind.

She puts out the almost unsmoked cigarette and hides her face in her hands.

– What is it?

She sobs and shakes her head. Then she blows her nose and scrapes the back of her head along the tiles behind her.

– You have nothing to do with it, but I have to get away for a while. The whole autumn has been one blasted mess. And now it looks like it's over with my boyfriend, I hope.

This is the first time she has mentioned her boyfriend. But I've had my suspicions.

- What is his name?

- His name?! That doesn't make a damn bit of difference . . . Besides, Ypsilon, you know that the professor has forbidden us to discuss our private lives with you!

- Get away for a while, what do you mean by that?

- That I take a couple of weeks vacation. I thought I'd better mention it. I'm afraid you're becoming too attached. Or that you'll get jealous. You really had no right to get so jealous just because I knitted that pointed beret for Flink!

- But you'll come back?

- I'll come back. Will you promise me something while I'm gone?

- First tell me what it is.

- No, promise . . . no, for that matter: I want you to cooperate, I want you to do your best. Don't be contrary. Things will go much better if you are not contrary. And you must trust us here. Everyone wishes you well. And I can assure you that the professor has your welfare very much at heart.

- One just feels a little deserted at times, there's no getting away from that fact.

- I know, we had a whole brain here before . . .

- Yes???

- Me and my big mouth! I've already said too much. There are those who have gone under owing to their own suspiciousness, Ypsilon. More I cannot say.

She hops down from the counter, throws her arms around the aquarium, and presses her right cheek to its front side. Mist from her mouth spreads out over the glass; a big, empty speech balloon.

29

Today I made my debut in the lecture hall. A maintenance man pushed me there in a wheelchair; evidently an ordinary cart was considered too unstable. I was conscious the whole time; thus one might say that this was my first real excursion from the laboratory building. We took the elevator down to the basement. It was delightful to experience the change in altitude in my organs of equilibrium. Once we got down to the basement, we went, via a tunnel, to a service corridor. A cement ramp led up to ground level. The light was overwhelming. I have, in any case, never before seen the Institute from the outside. It is an L-shaped building, three storeys high, of brick. The flat roof has many chimneys and ventilation ducts. The building is ringed by a park with round, polished hillocks; between the hillocks are some undernourished pine trees and tufts of grey grass. The sun stands low in the sky, making all the windows look like they need cleaning. Wherever there are shadows, snow remains; like sleep in the furrows of a drowsy person's brain. I cannot determine whether it is autumn or spring.

The sun is too strong for me. I call out to the maintenance man to ask him to lay a handkerchief or a newspaper over the aquarium. But he is not wearing the hearing-aid glasses. I make another attempt via thought transference. This does result in his taking out his handkerchief. But instead of covering me, he blows his nose.

The lecture hall is situated in a windowless pavilion at the other end of the park. When we roll in through the glass doors I don't see anything clearly; all I can see are pink shadows and violet circles that the sun has punched in my retina. I sense a dark corridor with coat hooks. We enter a high-ceilinged room - I sense more than see it. I have to wait there by myself for nearly a quarter of an hour. Slowly my sense of sight returns. Several tiers of empty seats stare up at me. Highest up, a little barricade fences off a projector. On one wall hang a couple of portraits in oils, on the other a soiled, old, original wall chart of Mendeleev's periodic table. The maintenance man returns with an older man in a grey coat. Together they lift me over to the long table that divides the actual area of the lecture hall from the long green blackboard.

After the hardships of the journey, I doze off for a little while. It can also be said that I am rocked to sleep. For a long time after the men have lifted the aquarium over to the table, the fluid inside it still arches in brief surges. At first they are so strong that I have to paddle with my ears to keep myself on an even keel in the choppy sea. I am awakened by the professor addressing me. I jump with a start; as usual, he has not adjusted the volume. His voice thunders through me as if I were the vaulted hall above a railway station.

- Good day, Ypsilon! Now you are going to meet my students.

The lecture hall is half-full. Younger people of both sexes sit scattered one by one or in small clusters. The two front rows are entirely empty.

- Now let's all of us start by moving down so we can see better, George says.

Reluctantly they move down. It is mainly the female students who responded to the request. When George begins to give an account of my background, my antennae are fully extended. But unfortunately, he has nothing to say that interests me. He entirely skips over what one calls the *antecedentia* and gets right into the technical aspects, the kinds of solutions I've been lying in and other such things. I understand that while I was still unconscious, I was transferred from bath to bath. I learn that the overshadowing problem in the beginning was my outer ears. To be able to move them, I require a small number of functional muscles. It has been shown that muscles have more difficulty doing without a regular blood supply than the brain itself has. They had to imbed a couple of extra electrodes in my ear muscles to get them going.

Then everyone comes forward and looks. It feels a bit solemn, almost as if I were Lenin himself in his glass coffin. How do I know that there is a corpse called Lenin and that it rests in an aquarium larger than my own? God, Darwin, Pavlov, Lenin, Hamlet . . . in whose palm I have rested? I have a whole wardrobe full of old names. Its door must have stood closed by mistake when they shot their electrical currents through my brain's house.

The students seem none too interested. They march by listlessly. A girl continues to work on her knitting while she's standing in line. One or another of them yawns halfheartedly. A boy takes out a pocketwatch and dangles it in front of my eye, presumably to see whether I can fix a moving object.

The lecture George subsequently gives is on learning and aggression. He starts with learning and the permanent changes that have been observed in brain cells following memory training. Not a particularly remarkable theory: he contends quite simply that I am a folded-over and crumpled-up phonograph record, or an interminable reel of recording tape, where every impression leaves its mark or its trace. I yawn and slowly begin to sink down toward the bottom of the tank by letting water trickle into the brain's interior hollows, those which function like swimming bladders. George notices this, of course, and taps his ring against the aquarium. I choose to resume my normal position. But it seems a bit unfair. Why shouldn't I be allowed to lie at the same sluggish level as the audience?

Then George says some lovely words concerning the concept of aggression. I don't have a notebook, as the students do. But I have something else: lots of unused memory tape.

Two neurosocial problems cause more concern than all the others, says George. The first problem is how to bring up the next generation on a sound neurobiological foundation. With our knowledge of the brain's growth periods, the question becomes one of what sorts of differentiated training to employ so that each individual can develop harmoniously and realize his genetic potential, regardless of whether he or she belongs to the great majority or the creative few. The second big problem touches on how to deal with the human tendency toward destructive aggression, which in the light of our current technological capabilities can destroy the human race. The human brain is an incredibly fine organ; it affords us the possibilities of solving complicated problems and planning for the future. Why do people who are so well equipped behave so irresponsibly? Is it possible that the basis for destructive aggression is part and parcel of the very organization of this superior brain? Nowadays, we actually know of a biochemical mechanism in man which can give rise to a level of aggression deadly to others. Now as before, an unsurpassed way to use knowledge correctly is expressed in the Greek motto *'gnothi seauton'* - 'know thy self', George says, and pauses for breath.

I lie there in all my glory, listening to this panegyric of my capabilities. I try to look friendly and inviting. I want the students, one after another, to come up to me and press their palms against the glass. Like an old gypsy, I will advise each one of them on his or her personal fate.

But instead there are mathematical exercises. During the pause, George and the maintenance man connect me to a computer storage device, so that I do not overexert my memory functions. I don't like having the apparatus on me. It's like giving dentures to someone who still has his own teeth. But I don't make a fuss. Quickly, but without much enthusiasm, first I play noughts and crosses with a student volunteer, then I beat George at chess in thirteen moves - to the undisguised delight of the students - and finally I solve some of the classical problems of mathematics, those which are part of the standard repertory.

With only five minutes remaining to the lecture hour, there's a question and answer period. The students fidget awkwardly, look up at the ceiling, pick their noses, or check their knitting instructions. Since nobody asks a question, they are all allowed to leave. This sets off a brief round of applause - and just as in the theatre, huge sections of the audience are already out in the cloakroom.

I relax, sink down to the bottom, and prepare myself for the return trip. Then a girl who has stayed behind comes up to me and George.

- What do you really intend to do with this, this . . . brain? she asks.

- He calls himself Clever, George answers.

- To what end will you use Clever?

- Basic research is an end in itself, George replies.

- But it must cost heaps of money. Do you mean that Biochine wants nothing in return?

- We in industry are just as interested in life's innermost secrets as at any university. But clearly, in the long run, we believe that this kind of experimentation will eventually come to serve mankind.

- How??

Now I'm all ears.

- How? George echoes. You can pretty well figure that one out for yourself.

- In that case I wouldn't be asking. Is it true that eventually you plan to let the brain tissue grow together with microcomputers' bubble memories, to develop a superbrain?

- That's something you've got from the sensationalist press, George says and laughs. But if it were so: do you think I would stand here and reveal industrial secrets? We don't invite you students to guest-lectures here only so that we can waste your time giving you information about the progress we're making in industry. We want to let you share in our basic research, that's all.

- And in the field of brain research, you are far ahead of the universities? Isn't that so?

- We are well ahead, if I may say so.

- Thanks! the girl says, shrugs her shoulders, gives me a crooked smile, and wobbles away on her high-heeled leather boots.

30

Things are still pretty much up and down for the most part. True, I no longer have to spend my days in the utility room, but the laboratory has changed somehow. The two long lab benches with their shelves and glassware have been ripped out. Instead, work has been done along the far wall, where the dog once had his cradle. Along that wall they have constructed a broad bench, led in extra water lines and drainage, and from the ceiling above it hang bunches of loose electrical wires; the free ends of the wires are wrapped in beige insulating tape. For several days, however, no work has been done. Since Emma is gone, I have no one to ask about it.

I am being taken care of by a variety of people. The only one whose name I know is the postdoctoral student, Curt. But I have difficulty with Curt, even though I know him by name. He is careless and impulsive. As long as he confined himself to taking apart the equipment, no great damage was done. But now the oscilloscopes and all the rest of the splendid things are gone. Thus there is no other object than I for his intensely curious fingers.

Flink, the chimp, is here again now, very keen on company, as usual. He plays two roles: if any of the personnel is present, he behaves like an irresponsible and unruly teenager - when we are alone he goes on interminably about his recollections. Actually, all he needs to get going is for the personnel to turn their backs. The advantage of sign language is that Flink can whip off a few sentences from the hip without anyone having the time to see.

- Now, we *are* agreed, aren't we? he says for the fiftieth time.

- Do you want it in writing?

- We have to deal with each other on the same terms, he emphasizes. I will tell you my recollections, and you will tell me yours. You are my memory bank, Ypsilon. If they run their erasers around inside my skull, I will come to you and withdraw my memory capital.

- And if you don't even remember that you have deposited your memory in me?

He becomes surly - or rather sad. After the insufferable beginning of our acquaintance, I still have a certain aversion to him. But of course he is deserving of all sympathy. So when he becomes sad, I have no reason to call him surly.

- Have I told you about the Island of the Apes?

- Yes. But we can certainly go over it again.

- Sure that I'm not boring you? If I am, just tell me so. Friendship demands honesty.

- That's all right, we can rehearse it. To be sure that I haven't forgotten anything.

Flink grabs hold of one of the bunches of cables that hang from the ceiling, winds it around his body, secures himself with his feet, and speaks with his long arms and hands while swinging slowly, with smaller and smaller arcs:

- Once upon a time there was a big war. Because of the war many important necessities did not reach the consumer countries. That's why people invented substitutes. Cars ran on producer gas, coffee was ground from roasted acorns. But it was even worse for scientists. Even in those days we anthropoid apes, especially chimps, were absolutely vital for research. Not the least for military research with its nerve gases and antidotes. To some extent we could be replaced with piglets, guinea pigs, or rabbits. But in some respects we were unique: pigs, guinea pigs, and rabbits cannot learn sign language. One cannot put a pig in a g-suit inside a satellite and expect it to manage

101

even the simplest of manipulations. But an ape can. Before the major transport routes were sealed because of the war, about twenty chimpanzees were moved from their natural habitats within the bounds of the savanna to a small, uninhabited island in an archipelago. Because we are all poor swimmers, neither fencing nor guards were necessary. They set up a row of kennels for protection against the rain, rigged up some old, weather-beaten equipment from a children's playground, and built sheet-metal containers, which were filled with food once a week.

Now Flink changes the direction of his motion on the bunch of wires so that instead of swinging from left to right, he goes forwards and backwards:

- I was born on the Island of the Apes. Every year a delegation of researchers came to test us young ones. The most intelligent of us came here or went to other labs or space-stations. The stupidest were disposed of via vivisection; those who were somewhere in between generally were sold to circuses or zoos. There wasn't much funding for the upkeep of the Island of the Apes. So it was a matter of raising money. We bright ones were taken from our parents early. I will not tell you about that day, no electrical shock in the world can obliterate that memory . . . You think it was all fun and games on the Island of the Apes?? No, Ypsilon, it was hell. Living beings need work. We had no work. In the jungle my parents were always busy gathering roots and leaves, guarding against jackals and snakes, carrying us little ones around, finding water holes, forecasting the weather or coaxing sweets from picture-taking tourists on safari.

No one needed to work on the Island of the Apes. No predatory animals threatened us. When it got cold, we went inside the kennels. The food was excellent, it contained both vitamins and vermifugal drugs. And the consequences, Ypsilon?? *Intrigues.* Love affairs, jealousy, acts of deception, blackmail, and mobbing. In the jungle the tribe had a set power structure, a strict pecking order . . . but the inequality had a purpose. In times of crisis, commands were obeyed. On the Island of the Apes there were no crises, no *external* crises. We couldn't do a thing about the humans taking some of our young away - at lions we could throw stones, but if we threw sticks or cones at the researchers, we risked immediate selection for demonstrating initiative.

- How much has Biochine paid for you?
- I have been sold in several stages. First I was at a breeding station. When I became sexually mature, they milked off some portions of my sperm for deep-freezing. They did that to each one of us.
- Then maybe by now you have several batches of children?
- No. The sperm will not be used until after I have shown what I am capable of, maybe not until after I'm dead, and when, with the help of some computer programme, my life can be summed up: worthy or not-worthy. But Biochine does not own my sperm; the university, or more specifically the genetic institute owns it. Nowadays, that's a very rich institution. No, I don't want to tire you out with details from the Island of the Apes. I don't want to relate too many of my boring reminiscences. Have you given any thought to this: if they set me back to zero and then I come back and ask you to tell me my life . . . have you considered that I now have the chance of a lifetime to doctor my background, to see to it that I only get happy and interesting memories in return?
- Isn't it important to you to know the truth?
- No, when I get old, maybe I'll want to be able to look back on a good life. Who can afford the truth, the whole truth I mean: you, perhaps? But, of course, you are a millionaire in the intelligence department . . . No, I don't blame you, I would not want to trade places with you. To hang here and swing in this tangle of wires gives me namely an indescribable feeling of bliss. You ought to be jealous of me, Ypsilon.
- I am.
- But I would like to tell you about something else I believe I have recalled. My parents could never forget Africa. Mother

often said: when the war is over you can bet I'll catch the first boat home. But the war had already been over a long time by then. Of course we all knew that. But not my mother, because she did not *want* to know. She would not have survived the knowledge: the war is over but I may not, in any case, go back. Do you know what place I long for? The Island of Apes, not the jungle; I would consider a return to the jungle a kind of sentimental journey to look for my roots. But to live in Africa? Never. The Island of the Apes with all its intrigues and its destructive idleness is the only home I know. And now here's something you'll be interested in hearing: in this very house there are several younger apes. They have never been either to Africa or to the Island of Apes. One of them was born in a grade-B circus that is always on the verge of bankruptcy. Of course that's where he longs to return. Another was born in an artificial womb. You ought to hear him embroider the tales of his childhood laboratory. If you walk up to him and start to talk about Africa, he bursts out laughing right in your face.

- If you were smart Flink, do you know what you should have told me about? You should have told me about how you grew up *here.*

- The problem with me is that I am a bad storyteller.

- Let me invent it then.

- You??

- I need something to occupy my wits. Let me make up a life for you, how you grew up here at Biochine. If it later becomes appropriate, if they set you back to zero, you can come here and get your life from me. A life that will make you never ever long for the Island of Apes. Your childhood home is here in any case!

- Should I leave my life in your hands? Completely?

- Think about it. What have you got to lose?

- Now I want you to tell me some things. You haven't uttered a sound about your own life.

He lets go of the artificial liana and sits down on the narrow ledge in front of the aquarium.

- I have no life to tell you about.
- But I know where to find it!
- Are you telling the truth?
- Your life is in a metal filing cabinet in the basement. A cabinet full of old documents and journals.
- I don't believe that. They are not so old-fashioned. If my life is to be found somewhere, if it has not - for reasons of secrecy - been utterly obliterated, then it is on magnetic tape or one of those newfangled antipodal bubble cards.
- Wrong, Ypsilon. I've been around this place long enough to know that the professor does not rely one hundred per cent on the machines. He is an old romantic. Haven't you noticed that? He has you in a filing cabinet.

31

They have set up screens so that I will not be 'disturbed' by the construction work in the far end of the laboratory. Of course I don't care for this, I am afraid that my suspiciousness will burgeon. This fear is shared by the research team. It was not long before they noticed that something was amiss. Every day they take samples of the water in which I rest. They check to see that the concentrations of nutrients and salts are correct - but they also check on my secretions. These last few days the 'paranoid titrations' have risen. We all know what that means: a charge is building up deep inside me.

But this time the research team has not tried to balance my growing suspiciousness with tranquillizers. Instead they have given me 'something else to think about' - with a little luck, this can have the same effect as psychopharmaceuticals. And we are, in any case, all of us uneasy about making me dependent on too many drugs. Instead they have given me a reading-machine. They have placed a slide projector beside me in the hood. In front of the construction workers' screens, a projection screen hangs from the ceiling. By breaking a photoelectric beam that goes through the aquarium, I can get the reading-machine going: page after page lights up on the projection screen. In the beginning, far too slowly. But now the image changes every three seconds. My denuded memory functions eidetically, that is to say, like a camera.

They still only allow me limited reading materials. Just now these are of three types: the good, old, department-store catalogues, musical scores, and textbooks on the central nervous system.

- The more you know about how you function, the calmer you ought to become, says the professor.

Maybe. But the process can work in precisely the opposite way: he who has seen the inside of a colour TV can easily get the impression that a thousand errors can arise at any time at all. Or if one thinks about one's own heart, about what an infinitely complicated process of coordination each heartbeat involves - does that make one calmer? But, actually, I think I have calmed down since I began to study. Nothing in the chemical analyses of my secretions contradicts this optimistic finding. It is comforting to know that the thinking part of the brain, the grey matter, has as many nerve cells or 'thought-cells' as the Milky Way has heavenly bodies. And that between these nerve cells, or neurons, there are 1,000,000,000,000,000 synapses or connections. Does one grow wiser knowing this? Who knows. Who can really say how much space a thought or a recollection requires. Flink's Island of the Apes, for example, does it take up a single nerve cell - or does it require a whole solar system? I asked the professor this morning. But he only laughed and said:

- And you ask that question of *us*. Shouldn't we really be asking it of you?

Does the brain exist for the sake of the body, or vice versa? None of the textbooks yet has answered that question, despite the fact that Biochine's library in this field ought to deal with analogous questions. If the brain exists for the body, then the brain should be seen as an appendage, one organ among many, a feedback and guidance system, a regulator or a relay without which the body would go into a spin, begin to boil, or dry out.

Maybe I am biased, but for me it is natural to think the reverse: the body I've left, wheresoever it now is, in a cemetery, a vat of formalin, a freezer, or in the form of a roving zombie - for me that body is nothing more than an elaborate costume. A system of prostheses and auxiliary motors to serve the brain, that is to say, me. In order to eat I need hands, a mouth, a stomach, and so forth. To get to the table I need legs. Almost all nourishment goes into the body, but to keep the brain at an acceptable glucose level - a brain eats only sugar - this intricate system is unnecessary, this vulnerable, difficult, bulky and stupid body. A body is stupid. Stupid as a root or the crown of a tree.

The brain, that is I. But *where* in the brain am I to be found? I asked the research team. As usual, when it comes to one of these all-embracing questions, it was the professor who replied:

- You know what, Ypsilon, I asked my former wife exactly the same question. Do you know what she said? She had never thought about it. For her the answer was obvious: somewhere inside the skull sat a little white figure who took care of everything, pretty much like a technician in front of the control panel in a nuclear reactor. And the little white figure was her 'self'.

A little white figure? Can that be any consolation for a mortal? Is it the little creature who abandons ship when one dies? And how exactly does that little white self inside there look? Does it have a brain, muscles, a stomach? Inside the brain of the little white one, maybe in turn there is another, even smaller figure, a green one, a tiny little old man who runs the whole show from his swivel chair. And so on through all the colours of the rainbow.

Sometimes in the evenings I lie down on my back here inside my brain. I lie comfortably with my hands under my head and my knees pulled up slightly. I lie and stare up toward my own skull's vaulting firmament. The ordinary images cannot be discerned: nowhere here are Ursa Major or the Pleiades, neither Orion's belt nor Canis Minor. But there are other patterns in this intricate embroidery, in this celestial canopy woven of axons. What a shame not to have paper, pencil, and a powerful telescope.

32

A delegation from the board of directors is coming to visit us. It has something to do with our subsidies. The rounds have been doubled; George makes rounds even in the afternoons. Am I making any progress? Am I profitable? Recently I have said virtually nothing at all. I would like to keep complete silence. But if I stop speaking altogether, my own life will be at risk. Then it is only natural for them to assume that something has gone wrong with one of my larger thought processes. I do not want to be thrown into the garbage disposal.

Management has informed us that their visit will take place after lunch. Two hours before lunch, the professor sat here and scratched my back. Tenderly, imaginatively, but methodically. Emma said, before she took off, that George has the reputation of being a lady-killer. But when I asked her point-blank, she denied having firsthand experience.

After the management luncheon, the visitors seem to be tipsy, sated, or sleepy from too much food. The management committee consists of seven people. Three of them are research scientists here in this building. They are not particularly interested, and while the professor talks and makes introductions, they take the opportunity to go over the page proofs of an article they're publishing. A layman on the board - going by his nametag, it seems he comes from personnel - asks about 'objectives'. From the looks on the researchers' faces and the grimaces they make at one another, I realize that the question shows but scanty understanding. But the professor explains patiently.

When I think it is my turn, it is instead the ventilation system that captures their attention. An older man on the board also sits on the Safety Committee. It turns into a long palaver. They bend over the aquarium without bothering about me. They run the beams of their flashlights around inside the ceiling of the hood above me.

Finally there is someone who takes notice of me. A short and plump, little woman with glasses on a cord around her neck:

- Ah, that he can live without companionship, she says, smiling - not at me but at the professor.

- A pure intellect hasn't very much use for social intercourse.

The other board members - excepting the men of science - look too. One makes a wry face. Another titters. I can well understand that I arouse uneasiness. No human being really wants to be confronted with his innermost self in this direct and brutal way.

When they march out of the laboratory, I feel utterly abandoned. Emma - why have you forsaken me? Entirely by my own hand, without the aid of any artificial means, I am on my way to sinking into a deep depression. Everything is meaningless.

After a few minutes have gone by, the professor comes in with his golf equipment. He gives me the thumbs-up and laughs:

- You took them by a storm, you rascal! The project was approved *and* funded.

- Don't drive me out of my mind! I say.

- That is exactly what we're trying to do, Clever. It's your mind we need. Not *you*.

Whistling happily, he marches off with his golf bag slung over his shoulder. The case's shape is like that of a heavy tube. As if made to carry a bazooka or a portable grenade launcher.

33

Last night the white rats came back. This was not at all like the impetuous prison break they attempted last time. How can I remember that there has been a last time? Clearly it's about time they did some housecleaning around here, in the form of electric shock treatments. It is no fun to have your past catch up with you. Recollections come mostly in the form of feelings. The predominant feeling is guilt. What am I really guilty of? Something dreadful - but what?

The rats were extremely polite. The first one - about two metres tall, walking on its hind legs with no difficulty whatsoever - first stuck the upper part of its body through the door at the left edge of my field of vision, smiled suavely, rapped its knuckles against the doorframe, paused there a few seconds, and then strode into the laboratory, making a gentle little bow first in my direction and then towards the screen, as if someone were standing concealed behind it. The rat tarried a while with its hands behind its back and looked all around, smiling. Then it cocked its head to one side, looked in my direction again, and made an enquiring gesture toward the door. I could not very well deny him permission to let in his companions. They came, walking with bent knees, almost on tiptoe, with awkward smiles, fully conscious of the late hour. They pointed out the various objects in the laboratory to one another. Their facial expressions could be summarized under the headings of wonder and admiration.

More and more came into the laboratory. I soon lost count.

They were all about two metres tall, a few may even have been close to two and a half. Even with all the crowding, one could see how the rats above all else were extremely careful not to come into contact with one another's whiskers. They casually trampled their neighbours' feet and drove their spindly elbows into one another's long bellies - but they looked out for their whiskers as if the hairs had been thin feelers made of glass. I identified with them. I am just as afraid for the two silver antennae on my crown as I am for my one eye.

What were all the rats doing in the laboratory in the middle of the night? I assume that they were a delegation. There were many of them, certainly more than 40. Only those who stood closest to my aquarium had a chance to look in.

The visit of the rats must have been purely routine. They really were very discreet. Not even the chief rat, the one who strode in first, dared to ask any direct questions. The whole group slowly walked around, looking; the majority of them with their small, rosy hands tightly grasping their whiskers. This produced a comical impression: they seemed to be carrying shimmering white sheaves of grain. I grew rather tired of the endless white fur and nodded off to sleep. I have taught myself a method of 'closing my eyes'. Instead of letting down the eyelid I do not have, I press my eye against the glass wall of the aquarium. When the eye is pressed, optical conditions change; the image splinters and is flecked with black spots. This is my way of shutting out the world around me. When I looked again, the whole delegation was gone; they had vanished as unobtrusively as they had appeared. They obviously didn't notice that they'd left behind a few isolated hairs and clumps of fur on the floor, and on sharp corners. If they had, I am certain they would have picked up after themselves.

I lie here contemplating the visit of the rats. The most striking feature was, after all, their size. Never before have I seen a laboratory rat that was longer than two tenths of a metre - excluding the tail - thus, these were ten times as long. But there is another explanation. Of course I know that George and company are in the midst of various experiments involving me. Sometimes they disconnect me and everything goes black - or, rather, white - for various lengths of time. It would be a mere trifle for them to move me to a much smaller room, to, let us say, a carefully constructed model of the lab a twentieth of its actual size. If they were to place such a dollhouse laboratory in front of my aquarium, would I then have any possibility whatsoever of deciding if the rats were two metres or two tenths of a metre?

34

They have completed the renovation. They have also laid down new tiles where the two lab benches stood. The new tiles are shinier than the old ones. Against the wall directly opposite me they have installed a new hood, which is wider and just slightly lower than mine. Inside it are shelves on which stand seven glass boxes of various sizes. A couple of them are about the same size as my aquarium, some are smaller, but one is at least twice as long. From inside the top of the hood hang connecting plugs, cords, wires, and spotlights, crowded together as in the theatre. Underneath the hood are four oscilloscopes; their windows tilt obliquely upward. There is also an ion pump, a transformer, and other electrical equipment.

Dismal prospects for the future? Are these new installations designed for me? The research team won't answer such stupid questions. In passing, I have learned from Flink that there's been talk of 'granule experiments' in the staff room. A concept which sounds harmless enough - but my readings in the year-book of *Advances in Neurophysiology* have given me some familiarity with the term. Granule experiments involve the injection of microcomputer chips, in the form of microscopic grains, into living tissue. Distinctions are made between 'granules' and 'rods': rods are microcomputers in the shape of hair-thin threads, which can be implanted into nerve fibres and aimed with precision towards certain centres or neural nuclei. Granules, on the other hand, are injected directly into the bloodstream, circulate with the corpuscles, and then settle down at various points in the central nervous system.

There are two important differences between granules and rods. Because of their enormous surface area, as compared to that of the granules, the rods have many times the storage capacity. But one cannot stick as many rods as one likes into a brain without causing injury to crossing or overlapping nerve-tracts. The problem with the granules is entirely different: to get them to land in the right places. The grains must be moulded in such a way as to fit into the neurons like the pieces of a jigsaw puzzle.

What both techniques have in common is the risk of rejection reaction. In principle, the benefits are also the same: the thinking tissue is relieved of a number of the more mechanical, sterotypic functions - learning and memory, for example.

I know that I am too expensive for the researchers to dare take any chances with me. It would take them months, maybe years, to train a replacement. And yet, I feel an instinctive horror of being treated with either granules or rods. I know this is a purely emotional reaction; in principle the technique is no worse than setting a pin into the neck of a broken femur. But I still cannot accept it. My intellectual life is as multi-tudinous and rich as the Milky Way. I do not want to have satellites or probes floating around up there. I do not want to have metal deep inside me.

This afternoon I got a new roommate in place of the dog. They brought in a refrigerated case and removed from it something I couldn't see; they were standing in front of it.

For several hours I have lain here trying to get a fix on my new roommate. But the distance between us - about seven metres - is a little too great. Was I ever nearsighted, or does the fluid in my aquarium distort the perspective? I begin to form a preliminary notion of my companion's appearance. In the faintly green, sparkling aquarium something pale pink is dimly visible. For the most part it lies just under the surface of the water, like a blurred lump; but sometimes it moves violently and with no apparent motivation whatsoever. When it moves, it looks like an octopus with short, fleshy arms that pump and swim. Evidently, its eyesight is poor, for when it makes sudden movements, it rams into the glass and rests there a few seconds, knocked out like a bird that has flown into a closed window.

It is a hand, a detached hand. This evening we were bathed, first I and then my companion. While I lay spanking clean, feeling as if I were resting between newly ironed, still damp sheets, I could follow in detail as Curt went over to the newcomer, put on a pair of rubber gloves, lifted it out of the aquarium, and put it in a towel. He came towards me and showed it to me: there lay a human hand, unnaturally white as hands always are when held under water for a long time. The hand was severed and sewn up just above the wrist. It raised an index finger straight up and groped in the air, as a snail with great suspiciousness extends its eye on its stalk after rain has fallen. He - or she - must be blind. After Curt put the hand back into the aquarium, he gave it an injection in one of the blue-green veins on its back. I assume this was food. With its thick skin, the hand certainly cannot absorb nourishment directly from the fluid which surrounds it. It gave a jerk when it got the injection, which indicates that it still has at least some part of its emotional life intact.

I do not know how I shall establish contact with the aimlessly drifting hand, which, for want of a better name, I simply call the Hand. With the chimp I can use sign language. Naturally, the Hand lends itself uncommonly well to sign language; nonetheless, it cannot see. But in some strange way light affects the Hand; otherwise they would not have aimed a spotlight on it. Evidently, some sort of phototropism comes into play; the nails turn towards the source of light. When the Hand knocks itself out after one of its sudden swimming excursions, it always lies with a half-closed fist in such a way that its nails form a ring of five squares facing the spotlight.

Can the Hand hear? On a couple of occasions it has turned its palm towards me and cupped itself, as one does when one is a little hard of hearing. But there just aren't any auditory organs to send sound to. I believe instead that the Hand's strength lies in its sense of touch. Sometimes it presses the tips of its fingers against the glass. If I had a foot I would stamp on the floor of my aquarium; if the Hand is sufficiently sensitive, it would certainly be able to pick up the vibrations. The Morse code does very nicely indeed, at least for me, who have a command of it. Why do I have a command of the Morse code? Did I once have a career in telegraphy?

It is remarkable that the Hand can move itself without any difficulty, even though it has been amputated from its arm. Many of the muscles for the fingers originate way up in the arm. More than likely, it takes almost no strength to speak of for a lone hand to move its own weight. The short finger-muscles seem to be enough. And the buoyant force of the water! Why keep a living hand under water if one does not want to make use of buoyancy? Polio victims, who cannot move themselves on land, often swim surprisingly well.

By mere chance I discovered how the Hand and I can correspond with each other. I often have these so-called phantom sensations: my back itches, my cheek twitches, or I feel pain in the hæmorrhoids that vanished long ago . . . Now, I felt an excruciating itch in the right ear that I still have. By pure instinct I moved the right hand I no longer have up towards that ear, stuck my middle finger into the auditory canal, and turned it back and forth. All the while I kept looking at the Hand; in practice I cannot really move my eye. Now I saw the Hand make exactly the same movement I experienced myself executing. It moved upward, bent the four other fingers but left the middle finger extended. Time after time the Hand turned the middle finger, as if it were a screwdriver driving in a screw. How wonderful it was to feel the pressure of a fingertip against the inside of my auditory canal!

35

Flink is back again, nagging me about our 'memory contract'. I do not want to hear about the Island of the Apes and jungles in Africa. I want him to get out of here. He disturbs my practice sessions with the Hand. Flink couldn't care less about the Hand. He regards it as an exotic starfish in a public aquarium. On no account will he help me try to make contact.

- Don't trouble yourself about the Hand, Flink signs. It is we thinking beings who must stick together!

- But we are sticking together! I promise you that I know your life by heart, each and every syllable, every single punctuation mark.

- But I know nothing of yours, except that you think you remember a woman in black who caresses your cheek when you're lying in a respirator. What is that compared to the Island of the Apes?

Of course it wouldn't take much skill for me to fabricate a life that would appease Flink. Maybe I could be an engineer in the space programme, with a wife and two school-age children. Maybe I could be an unmarried trapeze artist, who has fallen down from the roof of the tent and broken his neck. Or why not a mass-murderer, serving a life sentence under scientific supervision? There's a whole telephone book of lives to choose from. But I don't tell Flink any tall tales. It is far too simple to fall into my own trap: if they gave me a new series of shock treatments, Flink will be buzzing around here as soon as I have awakened. Then I'll gladly and uncritically accept my freely invented life story from the naive Flink.

- I have a present for you! Flink says, pulling out a green folder.

- A surprise?

- You might say that: your life.

Proudly he presses the folder's front side towards the glass of my aquarium. It reads YPSILON, Anamnesis, etc. For a moment I lose sight in my one eye. My field of vision constricts to a tunnel, as when one is about to faint. I also become dizzy and feel sick to my stomach. It is a little piece of good fortune that I am no longer connected to the oscilloscopes: the alarm would have sounded immediately.

- Where did you get hold of the folder?

- In the basement, in the filing cabinet I told you about!

- And how do you know that it is I?

- It says Ypsilon, as you can see. The same scrawl as on the piece of adhesive tape that's plastered on your aquarium. Here!

He scratches at the lower right corner of the glass between us. This is the first time that I learn that I have a name tag. They must have had fun at my expense after the first series of shock treatments, back when, for a while, I thought my name was Clever.

Flink begins to leaf through the folder. It is thick, between 100 and 200 pages. The text flickers by, EEG-curves, lab-test results, codes.

- Why didn't you steal your own records? I ask. Then you wouldn't need to rely on me, on my remembering your childhood.

First he pretends not to hear. When I repeat the question he becomes embarrassed.

- The fact is I can't read. No more than a few signs.

All along I have taken it for granted that Flink can read - too rash a conclusion. He who has a command of sign language, of course, need not be able to read letters. An illiterate can, in any case, be a very good speaker without even being able to read his own name.

- If I could I would read your records to you, Ypsilon.

- I'm glad that you can't read.
- But I have another idea. I can sneak in here with a few pages at a time and press them up against the aquarium in front of that eye of yours. You certainly read faster than any human being . . . Or if you want I can try to get photocopies made that you can put in the reading-machine.
- They've taken away the reading-machine. They weren't sure it was doing me any good.
- Then I don't know what we'll do. But if we hurry now, surely you'll have time to read two or three pages?
- I'm going to ask you something very important; I want you to promise to do what I ask of you now.
- Sure thing.
- I want you immediately to go back down to the basement and stuff the folder back into its filing cabinet.
- When I've had so much trouble swiping it?! And when I've already found the perfect hiding place for it: behind the toilet tank in the john.
- Put it back. They will discover that it's gone!
- They sure as hell won't suspect me, a stupid ape!
- I implore you.
Now he is sad. Dejectedly he flips through the folder as through a bundle of notes which have suddenly been devalued to a fraction of their previous worth.
- If only I understood why?
- Because I can't manage it, I say. You know there is no turning back. I cannot stand hearing about a life . . . Maybe I have children, Flink. But I do not want to know. I simply cannot. Besides, my continued existence here depends on my cooperating. What do you think will happen to me if the professor discovers that I have read my own case history? Shock treatments again.
Flink grows anxious and changes the topic; instantaneously he swings from abject disappointment to enthusiasm:
- I know what they intend to do with you!!
How can Flink know this? He cannot even read.

- They want to make an example of you!

- How?

- If you weren't lying here you'd be dead, no? And if they take care of you properly, you ought to be able to live 800 years?!

- Just about.

- But don't you see, Ypsilon: You are the winning ticket for the scientists! You are of no direct practical use to them, but you are an *example*. You see, you demonstrate that if science spends enough money, spends it correctly, death can be overcome. Or in any case warded off for 800 years! And that is just what you human beings want to hear from scientists: that science can keep the Grim Reaper locked up in the shed!

- A lovely theory, Flink . . .

- Ingenious! Admit it.

- But wrong. Why, in that case, do I get shock treatments for my memory? Why speech-training? Why all this anxiety when my IQ fluctuates? Why these expensive antennae? If it were only a matter of showing that a brain can be kept alive, why then should they *risk* that life with complicated operations? You are wrong, Flink.

- Excuse me. It is distressing to be put in one's place; it's painful to realize that one is not as clever as you . . .

- I believe that they have something quite special in mind for me. I am too costly to be nothing more than a sideshow in a circus. Biochine is a serious company - their shareholders demand returns on their investments.

Flink yields to this economic marketplace reasoning, jams the green casebook under his arm, nods, and slinks out.

There are other reasons why Flink's theory does not hold. They have begun to treat me with small doses of cortisone. First I didn't pay any attention to it. But when I began to feel swollen and sometimes found myself in the throes of an inexplicable anxiety and had nightmares to boot, I asked when they made their rounds. Yes, they were giving me cortisone, a hormone produced in the adrenal glands. Why? I got nothing but evasive answers. But they underestimate me: I believe they are preparing to transplant me. In order to accomplish this, they have to get my own immune system under control.

Where can they possibly transplant me? Do they intend to sew me into the body of some head-of-state with hardened arteries? I would prefer to return to my old body. Maybe they have repaired it while I have been lying here. I would so like to go home to my old brainpan, just as a young bird longs to return to its nest. Fantasies! But there is absolutely no need to suppress the immunological defences of one who is to be transplanted back into himself.

36

It is Saturday and I have this frantic itching throughout my body. I swim around like a frightened perch in my tiny basin. I'm looking for a partner. Male or female - makes no difference, as long as it is a living creature, one I can mate with. I cling close to the glass and rub the stump of my medulla up against the hard surface. The postdoc, who has just given me food, sticks his finger into my tank; but hurriedly retreats from the field in terror when I ardently attack his finger.

What's got into me?! I cannot remember at any time during my stay here being so entirely consumed with lust. Though I must be on guard against my own memory, which they've blasted away. But one can certainly recognize one's own feelings - no need of a cataloguing system for that. Covetously I stare at the Hand in the aquarium opposite me. Shall I go down to the bottom of my tank, pump myself full of energy, take a running leap and shoot up like an underwater missile, sailing straight across the room to tumble down and land right in the delicious crease between the hand's thumb and forefinger?!

Pornographic pictures run through my brain. Instincts whip me around and around in the aquarium. I lie belly-up in the water and offer up my crevices and holes. But no one comes to relieve me. By the skin of my teeth I manage to turn myself right side up again - I do not want to lie here like a helpless beetle and drown in my own juices. Giddily I toss and turn down towards the bottom like a coin in a fountain. Then I catch sight of George. What is he doing here on a Saturday?!

- There, there, Ypsilon, he says, lowering in his whole hand.
I push and prod against his palm until a slow spasm travels through me.
- Is that better now?
I nod, all tired out; my ears are limp too.
- A little mistake. The postdoc happened to give you some of the testosterone that was meant for one of the capons in the hen house. It will soon pass.
So I've had a dose of sex hormone. All I need now is for adolescent acne to break out all over my exterior.
- Can't you ask first? I say. Now that we can speak with one another. Let me in on things so I can check the labels on the bottles!
- We'll give it some thought.
George has brought along a large case with feminine curves; it can hardly be for golf clubs.
- Would you like me to play a little for you? he asks and unpacks a cello.
I grow happy. George takes a stool, screws the pin into the bottom of the cello, rosins and blows the dust off the bow, tunes the instrument, looks up at the ceiling, raises the bow with a flourish, bends himself over the cello, and plays.
It is very beautiful. Since I have two antennae I can hear the piece in stereo. Music fascinates me. I know that for a long time I believed one had to summon up images in one's imagination while listening. That became very tiresome, and I quickly got lost among the jumbled rubbish heap of images. But not too long ago - how long? - I discovered that one needn't bother oneself with pictures. Instead one should take the theme to oneself, into oneself, and follow it; no illustrations, no disturbing associations.
George dries his hands on a handkerchief, closes his eyes, makes up his mind, and begins the next piece. He has a professional touch with the cello. What a many-sided talent: brain professor, golf player, and cellist! At the conclusion of the second piece, a vigorous but slightly fumbling round of applause

can be heard in the laboratory. Flink has come in and seated himself on an oscilloscope without my noticing. Because it is Saturday, he is not wearing a white coat. Instead his only stitch of clothing is a chic silver necktie, knotted around his non-existent neck. He applauds with long arms and grins with unsavoury tusks.

I, too, want to applaud! Partly because it is lovely, partly because now there's a contest between Flink and myself. Which of us does George like best? With all my might I pretend to applaud. First with my ears, but that feels unnatural. Then with my non-existent hands. Then I catch sight of the third member of the audience, who is showing George his appreciation. It is the Hand. Because it is alone, it cannot applaud in the usual manner, only clap against the side wall of the aquarium. The more I devote myself to my fantasies of applauding, the more powerfully the Hand moves. The water splashes high, so high that George puts the cello down and spreads his white hand-kerchief over the Hand's aquarium. Flink and I, of course, smoulder with jealous rage as a result. I decide to applaud even more forcefully after the next piece.

The professor goes on playing until he is dripping with sweat. But neither Flink nor I are listening any longer. Instead we keep an eye on each other to see who will be the first to applaud. I win, I am quicker on the uptake than a half-educated chimp. But: no sooner have I got going than the Hand starts in! The Hand claps so zealously that the white handkerchief sails down into the water and winds itself around a couple of fingers. The Hand is transformed into a drowning person who, in a last attempt to call attention to himself, holds up a fluttering handkerchief.

At the same time, my own applause slackens, goes into slow motion. I stop abruptly. The Hand stops, too. I applaud vehe-mently. The Hand applauds as vehemently as the handkerchief permits. So it really is I who am applauding via the Hand; it is entirely under my influence. I had of course noticed similar tendencies earlier. But now obedience is total! I wriggle out of the handkerchief; I flick at the surface of the water so that it splashes on Flink - I clench my fist as a sign of victory.

George, who has bowed politely to Flink, notices that something unusual is going on. Flabbergasted, he stares at the Hand's movements. I stop at once and let the Hand sink. It is not worth revealing too much. They have control of my memory. But I don't intend to let them get at my ability to control the Hand.

37

The blind usually have guide dogs. But I am not blind - what then shall the Hand be called? Not my sighted German shepherd, the Hand is rather my finger in the pie. It is evening. The staff has gone home and I concentrate on the Hand. It lies right across from me in its aquarium. A birdcage stands on the shelf below. They only keep the Hand in the cage for short-distance journeys.

- Wave! I think, and the Hand waves.

This looks a little odd, since the Hand has no forearm from which to swing. It looks more like it's trying to attack the glass in front of it.

- Climb up! I think, and the Hand begins its arduous attempt to get over the rim of the aquarium. This is not easy because there isn't even a board from which it might jump. Once upon a time there was a frog that landed in a bowl of cream. The sides were too slippery to climb up. And there was no ledge to hop from. But the frog did not give up; he swam round and round until the cream turned to butter and he could jump off the buttery clump. But what does one do with a detached hand in a glass tank filled with slightly saline water? One cannot very well expect the Hand to churn the sea into butter.

Above the Hand's aquarium, there is a white plastic container with a reserve supply of water in it. When the water level in the aquarium sinks, a valve opens automatically. I make the Hand paddle water away from the water-level gauge in order to fool the gauge. In this way we raise the water level almost to the rim. Now the Hand can get two of its fingers' top joints over the edge of the glass and begin to pull its way out. It works! With a dull thud the Hand falls down from the aquarium on to the roof of the birdcage. It remains lying there for a while. When it revives, it climbs down from the cage and then farther down. I can no longer see it. But I draw it to me like a magnet. It is wandering somewhere on the tiled floor. All the time I feel us drawing closer to each other. The fingers find a tube and begin to climb upward; the Hand reaches a shelf and approaches sideways, like a crab. When the Hand suddenly stands right in front of me in the hood, I am bursting with triumph.

The following night I have the Hand repeat exactly the same exercise. We cannot take any risks. It would be particularly catastrophic if the Hand did not make it back to its home. If it got stuck behind a radiator or piece of equipment, or got trampled to death by the nightwatchman. If it is not back in time for its morning meal - which it must take in the form of an injection - it will soon be afflicted with gangrene and die.

Night after night. The same schedule. But on the seventh night we feel ready. A couple of doors away, just next to the staff room, lies the office of the secretary. Each time I have been taken out of the aquarium, I have tried to learn something new about my surroundings. On the seventh night I send the Hand to the office. Since it cannot see, we have to try to orientate ourselves using feeling and intuition. In my solitude I have especially cultivated the latter on the exposed surfaces of my brain. Not only do I have a sixth sense, I have the beginnings of a seventh and an eighth as well. In the secretary's office the Hand's mission is to swipe a pen, a pad, an envelope, and if possible, postage stamps.

One night it comes lugging an envelope, which it proudly lays before me. Together we admire our catch for nearly an hour before we have to set to hiding it. We hide it under my aquarium. Between the bottom of the tank and the tiles of the hood, there's a crevice half a centimetre high. The following night, the Hand comes with a pen, which, however, is too thick to insert in the crack. The Hand has to take the pen with it and stick it in the sawdust at the bottom of the birdcage. Finally we steal a telephone message pad. That's something we cannot hide. We let it lie out in the open where anybody can see it and depend on the general sloppiness of the staff. The two part-time temporaries don't appear especially ambitious.

In the nights that follow we practise the noble art of penmanship. The first week's results are dreadful. Since it hasn't got an arm, the Hand must guide the pen over the message pad's very small pages, dragging itself along as well. The Hand staggers under the weight of the pen like an overloaded caber thrower. Another problem, one I foresaw but underestimated, is what to do with all the smudged paper. We can't very well leave it lying around. We solve the problem by having the Hand, en route home, make a detour into the room next door, where it lets the rats eat up the pieces of paper.

After a week our handwriting is just barely legible. But to whom shall we write? Shall we write to the radio station and request a particular record? Shall we write to someone in authority and complain about our care? Pointless. Biochine is part of an international cartel. We must assume that George and the firm act in accordance with whatever legislation has been passed. And if they don't, surely they have lawyers who can make excuses for them.

One night I decide that we should get ourselves a pen pal. Together we compose an ad for the personal column. We write:

INTELLECTUAL MALE, 40ish, single, honourable intentions. Seeks like-minded partner for companionship, marriage.

The next night we finish the letter and seal the envelope - which did not prove to be the simplest part. Now all that's wanting is a stamp. I know they are kept in a metal box in the office - but, unfortunately, the box is locked. While waiting for a stamp, we stuff the letter into the hiding place under my aquarium. It feels as if life is at last beginning to open up.

The next night the Hand pulls out the letter. And lets the rats eat it up. I don't want a like-minded partner! I want Emma to come back.

38

Today I am present in the staff room during the afternoon coffee break. They carried me here on a cabinet door. This way the water didn't slosh around so much in my tank, and the risk of seasickness declined. Now they have placed me at one end of the coffee table. On the other end stands a large cake. Between the cake and me there's a vase of dried flowers. The bouquet obscures my view of the cake itself. But the slender, rose-coloured candles stick up over the flowers. There are 21 candles on the cake. At the head of the table, the birthday child sits in a highchair. It's for Flink, it's the chimp's birthday today. I'm a little surprised he's invited me. We really shouldn't show that we are friends.

The white rats have not been invited, but the Hand has been. The Hand is locked up in an ordinary parrakeet cage, which they've set next to my aquarium. The Hand does not seem to be particularly interested. It scratches around calmly in the sawdust at the bottom of the cage.

George is not here - though I'm sure he's invited. The birthday address is given instead by the veterinarian, who is chiefly responsible for Flink. I know him only slightly. The speech he delivers is gloomy, but, one may presume, deeply felt:

- My dear Flink, the veterinarian says with his nose in his script, for a chimpanzee, twenty-one years is not as insignificant as it sounds. For a human being it implies the end of his schooling. For a chimpanzee it means standing at the threshold of the golden years of middle age. For you Flink, life does not begin at forty, it begins at twenty. As we all know, there is much, a great deal, to be said for the golden years into which Flink now prepares himself to enter. But let me seize the opportunity also to be a little *serious*. For many people, those who have not put their houses in order, middle age is not the highpoint in the arc of their lives, but rather a dead-end. Let me tell you the story of the middle-aged man who strove upwards all his life. He experienced his life as a long, steep stairway, winding through dark vaults. High up at the top of the stairs he could perceive a source of light, as if the stairway opened onto a sunlit roof terrace with leafy trees, flowers, and purling spring water. His goal in life was to reach these hanging gardens as quickly as possible, gardens he imagined to be a Paradise on Earth. Night and day he struggled upward, step by step. And one day in the middle of his life he stood on the threshold of the light-filled opening and prepared to set foot in the roof garden. But when he ascended the final stair, he came up against a sheet of glass that barred the stairway. And this was no ordinary sheet of plate glass, my friends. It was a mirror! The light which he thought was the future actually was only a reflection from the tunnel's entrance.

Now I raise my coffee cup in a toast to you, Flink. We all raise our coffee cups to the birthday child. Because we are convinced, Flink, that your goal in life never has been an illusory mirror. You are a person who, even while standing with both feet firmly planted on the ground, has always looked up toward the sky, the free, blue veritable heavens!

Everyone around the table - the veterinarian, the postdoc, and one of the cleaning women who suddenly has been called away from her work - has tears in his eyes while toasting Flink. Flink himself blubbers so much that concentric ripples splatter in my aquarium. Then the vet gives him the present for which everyone has contributed. It is a Polaroid camera.

- From all of us! the vet says emphatically, but I myself have not chipped in; and I rather doubt that the Hand has either.

Then it is time for Flink to blow out the candles on the cake.

This becomes an awkward situation. His mouth is far too broad, his lips far too stiff, and they can't quite manage to do their duty. Jets of air hiss out in all directions and from all sides: one stream takes with it some of the cream on the cake; another overturns a couple of dried, featherweight flowers from the squat vase.

The postdoc wants to help by placing himself obliquely behind Flink's chair and blowing. But it occurs to me that I ought to intervene: I stare right into the postdoc's brow and inspire an idea in his brain. He catches on almost at once and executes my will: letting the Hand out of the birdcage. Then I guide the Hand on its spidery walk towards the cake. Once it has reached the cake, I make it take a few quick leaps and lunges at the small lights. Hastily the Hand snuffs out the flames between thumb and forefinger, extinguishing them.

The Hand slinks back into the cage; Flink gets the first piece of cake and stuffs it crosswise into his jaws. Then he greedily sucks his black fingers clean. He's given a second piece and crams it in before the others have had a chance to distribute the remaining slices. Chuckling contentedly, Flink leaves his highchair, swings himself up to the ceiling lamp, and starts to photograph us with his new Polaroid. He climbs all around the room to find new angles: atop the bookshelf, on the exhaust fan for the stove, on the curtains, and finally he straddles the aquarium and fires off a flash right into my cerebral cortex.

No sooner has Flink taken the pictures than he immediately wants to tear them out of the camera, without waiting the prescribed period of time. But the vet persuades him to wait. When the pictures are ready, Flink is not at all satisfied with them. He tears them up and, from his perch in the ceiling lamp, throws the pieces all over the table.

Then a film is shown. Flink has put in a request for his favourite film, *Koko: A Talking Gorilla*. It is almost one hour long and shows how a female scientist teaches sign language to a young female gorilla. One can follow in detail the trials and tribulations not only of the researcher, but also, and not least, of Koko. I grow bored, and instead of watching the film, I let the Hand run a couple of warm-up laps around the inside of the cage. I want to test its muscular strength. The Hand has adapted itself to dry land in an almost miraculous way. Without any further assistance from the buoyant force of the water, it can perform complicated manoeuvres which require good muscle tone.

When the film is over, Flink goes around the table and embraces everyone. Suddenly he throws the camera right at the vet. In the next instant he tears at the curtains and kicks at the window. But he doesn't make a hole in the windowpane. Instead, he swings over to the door. But it is locked. Everyone stands astonished and speechless. Flink cowers in a corner under the window seat, his crooked, old-man's back towards us.

The veterinarian begins to laugh. The others join in. In a flash Flink is up on the window seat. He laughs so hard that his tears splash down. Then he starts to applaud and does not stop until everyone in the room is applauding.

Now the professor appears in the doorway. Behind him an assistant surgeon waits. The vet takes Flink by the hand and leads him over to the professor. The professor lifts Flink up onto his arm and strokes his coconut-head. Flink looks at us, sniggers panic-stricken, and waves his long arm at us. His overly long bib hangs down in front of his body like an apron.

39

They are preparing something. They have taken the Hand's
aquarium into the utility room. Yesterday three men were busy
for more than 13 hours setting up a closed-circuit security
camera where the emergency shower once stood, that is to say
on the wall to the left from my point of view. The emergency
shower vanished when the laboratory benches did. Because they
no longer keep any acids or corrosive chemicals here, an
emergency shower is no longer necessary. The little grey camera
with its flashing lens is mounted on a movable arm: the camera
slowly sweeps back and forth over the laboratory. It takes 20
seconds for it to start at the far wall, pass over me, turn, and
go back. When I asked about it during rounds this morning, the
professor said:
  - The insurance company made us install it. You see, someone
broke into our casebook file last Wednesday.
  But they aren't satisfied with the camera alone. All morning
there's been lively activity at the far wall. The postdoc Curt
has been in his element. They have calibrated and tested the
four oscilloscopes. Just now the electricians are on their break.
Curt is outside making a call to the camera company. From what
I can understand, some sort of unfortunate interference has
arisen between the closed-circuit camera and the oscilloscopes.
They disturb one another.
  The electricians - two young men about 18 years of age -
each sit on a stepladder, eating fried-egg sandwiches and staring
at me. Between mouthfuls they talk about me. One of them says

this is all very interesting. The other one is upset. He's thinking of telling his pastor about me when he gets home. The first one reminds him of his pledge to keep silent. But the second one doesn't give a damn about it. The Church cannot allow people to keep a live human brain in a can of water. This must be against nature. Lots of things are against nature, says the first electrician. But there has to be an absolute limit, is the answer he gets.

Curt rushes in, looking worried; his coffee spills from its paper cup, forming a light brown star on the tiled floor. The electricians go on chewing. Curt looks at the clock. The electricians also look at the clock - and sink their teeth into their respective slabs of grilled herring on crispbread.

Some hours later there are six people in the room: three from the camera company, who attend to the camera, plus Curt and the electricians, who busy themselves with the oscilloscopes. They continue working, even until it begins to grow dark outside. Then the professor and my psychiatrist enter. But they take no notice of me whatsoever. They ask and look, point, poke, enter figures, and carry on discussions. The camera people leave. People from the surgery unit come in, rolling a huge aluminium cylinder, which has an opening on top. It rotates like a cement mixer. Fumes also issue from the cylinder: heavy, white clouds of carbon dioxide gas that drift around their legs like a coiling bridal veil.

Now the electricians are also free to go home. Those who remain put on masks and bone-yellow rubber gloves. Using a long pair of tongs, a nurse takes green surgical cloths from a steaming metal box and makes a bed in one of the empty aquariums. She also clamps additional cloths around the opening of the cylinder. Then Curt calibrates the oscilloscopes one last time. A technician comes panting with a white box, which I recognize as an EEG-machine. Finally they seem to have finished. Everyone turns his face up towards the clock on the wall. Then the professor's hands dive down into the cylinder. They emerge with something whose form resembles an ostrich egg. Steam rises around the cooled-down 'egg'. I cannot see in detail what they are doing, I'm only guessing from their movements. The professor works in the aquarium while Curt adjusts the wires and contacts in the ceiling of the hood. An assistant rolls the cylinder away. The nurse takes a step back and loosens her facemask. She's about the same age as Emma. The surgical attire gives her face an austere beauty.

The team works through the night. A few get to go home just past midnight; but the professor, the psychiatrist, and Curt remain. Just before four, evidently some sort of crisis occurs. Curt has to telephone for the surgical staff again, who come running after a few minutes, their faces swollen with sleep, and frantically massaging their fingers to restore feeling in them. After some hours the situation has stabilized. Curt gets coffee and the psychiatrist produces a camera with a flash attachment. She takes several pictures from various angles. Suddenly she turns around and fires off a shot at me too. My eye becomes empty and white from the whiplash of light. Several minutes, maybe even a quarter of an hour, pass before I can see. By then they have gone. It begins to get light outside. The 'ostrich egg' in the aquarium right across from me is no longer white. It is yellowish-grey and cleft along its centre line. All is quiet and the oscilloscopes' various curves billow sluggishly, like eels standing in a gentle stream. The Hand has also returned and is back in its usual place, one shelf below the newcomer. The closed-circuit camera makes its long sweeps, like a lighthouse beacon. I focus on the newcomer. It is like seeing oneself in a mirror. Down left on the front of the aquarium, a broad piece of pink adhesive tape is plastered. The text, in felt-tip marker, reads: OMEGA.

40

I'm beside myself with happiness: with a smile on her lips, Emma
has returned. Tanned, talkative, lovable. She has been on vacation.
She is absolutely certain that she told me about it before. She did
tell me she'd be gone - but not that she would be travelling. But
I can't go on sulking about this point; she left in good faith -
and now she's back. Both of us are radiant with happiness, but I
feel very pale beside her.

This morning I had an eminently proper bath. The substitutes
who have been taking care of me in Emma's absence were not
entrusted with the task of bathing me. I'm thankful for that; I
don't want to be dropped on the floor. Today I've also had my
first shower. We let the stream of water run down a couple of my
hanging cerebral nerves so that I would get to know how it felt.
A delightful spring rain!

Everything's done now, and I eagerly ask Emma to sit down and
tell me about her vacation. She wants to go and change clothes
first, but I implore her: sit, just for a moment. She sits down and
leans her forehead against the aquarium. Her tanned skin becomes
dough-white where it comes into contact with the glass.

- Did you travel alone, Emma?!
- There were two of us.
- Who??
- A friend. Girls don't travel by themselves, not to those kinds
of places.

No, of course not. How silly of me. If I'd known she'd gone
alone on a Mediterranean vacation, I would have been very

worried about her.
- Did you get my postcard?
- What postcard??
- The one I wrote to you.
- I haven't had any mail at all. But you, of all people, should know: I'm never allowed to get any mail!
- That's just what I was thinking of trying to change. The card will probably come any day now.
- What did you do in the evenings?
- Calm down, now, Ypsilon. We spent the days on the *playa*. From ten till two. And then again from four until nearly seven.
- Are you that brown all over your body?
Though she points a finger to scold me, she doesn't look at all stern; rather, she looks happy, as if she'd been given a compliment. She goes on to tell me about the ice-cream man, the man who rented out boats, the old woman who sold lace, and the loud Germans who were all over the place. She didn't go swimming in the sea; it was too cold and dirty. One could ride a pedal boat in the sea. They went swimming in the pool.
- Was there a lot of chlorine in the pool? Do you think I could have swum around a while there?
My big problem is my shyness. What I really want to call out to Emma is 'Crawl in with me.' But I will say it - before this day has ended.
- And what did you do with yourselves in the evenings?
- Not so fast. We've only come as far as lunch now. We made our own lunch. Bought smoked ham, eggs, fruits and vegetables that we fixed ourselves. We had our own kitchen. Or more like a kitchenette.
- Was it sunny all the time?
- Two days it was cloudy, and one night it thundered like the devil. Now I have got to go and change my clothes. See you at coffee!
She leaves. I have enormous difficulty putting a damper on my expectations. This afternoon I will ask her. *Que sera, sera.* I know that she accepts me, that she's not scared off by my extraordinary

appearance. People only care about each other's appearance in the beginning of a relationship; later on they don't give it a thought. Well, of course, I think about how Emma looks. It's not just that she's so nicely tanned. She also seems to have matured, her cheeks are more drawn, firmer, sharper. It suits her.

Several hours slowly pass before she comes back. I lie and glare at my roommates: the Hand and Omega. Of course Emma has much more work to do than usual, with the rats, and other things. Has she sent a postcard to the rats too? A thick, fibrous card that is gnawproof.

When at last she returns, she is wearing a new red dress with small gold checks. She has a turquoise scarf in her hair. She holds her hands in her dress pockets like a fashion model and swirls around in front of me. For want of hands I applaud with my ears, which makes waves in the aquarium. For several minutes afterwards I lie and rock and see the world sliced up and distorted. Emma is carried away in big, garish, art nouveau blotches.

She sits with her chin resting on one of her hands. With the other she strokes the glass between us, as if trying to calm the agitated water.

- And did you go dancing in the evenings?!
- In the evenings we went out to eat, she says haughtily.
- How were the prices?
- About half of ours. Wine cost no more than milk.

Wine? I know that I've drunk wine. When?? Just now I'm dying to have some wine, some champagne. I wish she would empty a half-bottle into the aquarium. I would like to feel the small, tingling bubbles climb up my recesses and canals.

- But afterwards, you must have gone out dancing?
- Curiosity killed the cat!
- Didn't you even go to a discotheque?
- Now, I have to go home. To be continued, tomorrow!

There I lie with my offer: crawl in with me! Perhaps it is just as well to let such a decisive question go until my morning bath. She has promised to give me a shower tomorrow too.

41

They have divided up the workload here. To my great disappointment, Emma is in charge of the new brain, Omega, while Curt takes care of me. They even work different hours. Emma comes in on schedule, punctually at seven in the morning. But Curt comes when he likes. He has his own research to do and that comes first. As soon as Emma is within range, I implore: Sit a while - surely you can sacrifice a coffee break?! But she shakes her head and hurries along to the rats, the Hand, and Omega. In addition to these duties she must also buy the Danish pastries for the staff room; the secretary has a breast abscess and is home on sick leave.

Curt saunters in with his coat unbuttoned; between the hem of his crumpled T-shirt and the waist of his sagging jeans, half of his hairy belly is in plain view. His clogs strike hard against the tiled floor so that the surfaces of all the liquids in the laboratory start to quiver. Without observing any of the niceties, he lifts me up out of the aquarium and inspects my convolutions with a worn magnifying glass, covered with fingerprints.

- You're a damned good listener, Einstein, he says, spraying me with a little distilled water.

- Don't call me Einstein! I say once he's plopped me back down into the aquarium.

Then he jabbers at me. Am I listening? I have no choice. Indeed, I can dream myself away. But if I do that, I suddenly lose track of where the sound of his voice is coming from. He moves around in the room while he talks. I have to know where he is.

141

That's why I handle each of his words with the greatest of care. They come tossing through the fog like life buoys. When he gets around to the topic of his research, I'm all ears. I don't want to lose his last footstep or the scarcely discernible sound of the elevator doors.

- You are my father confessor, he says apologetically, after having dropped me so carelessly into a bowl that I landed straight on top of my eye.

My blinded eye hurts and throbs. Curt dabs it with a compress that has been saturated with painkillers.

- Damned bad luck, Einstein, tumbling right on your eye, he says. He's worried about his research, which has ballooned. First it was only a matter of a short paper. Now it's on the way to becoming a book.

- A ten-year plan, he says tiredly. George thinks it's marvellous. He believes we're on a hot trail. I don't agree. I don't want to spend my life buried in cybernetic simians. Do you know what I'd like to be working on? The will. Why do we go around 'willing' all the time? I believe a hitch occurred at some stage of evolution. Someone forgot to turn off the tap, as they say. No, just think about the alternative: if one could portion out the will in small doses. Turn the gas on all the way when necessary - and at no other time. None of this going around in circles all the time. Damn, I myself know only too well what a drag it is. To keep one will under control, you always have to set another one, an opposing one, in motion. Otherwise you capsize. Nature couldn't have meant it to be that way. Nature is thrifty, Einstein. Why should one have a complicated feedback system when it isn't necessary? I would like to construct a valve for the will. Open or closed. None of this damned, half-hearted . . . Do you know what George says? He thinks this is an *interesting idea*. But hard to research. Yes, of course he's right, but I want to do something really big, don't you see?! Though there's no grant money for that. On the other hand, the funding possibilities for experimentation with cybernetic simians are seemingly limitless. The cartel has put a high priority on mechanized monkeys. What manpower!

Repeating the same task over and over again until someone says stop. The only drawback is that they can burn themselves out, burst themselves when they're working with something too heavy. And they need care. George wants me to think up some sort of early warning system. When apes have their good, old brains, they can sense an accumulation of lactic acid in their muscles. They feel pain. But when their brains have been replaced by relays, by microchips, this doesn't work. Someone has to invent a device that measures the level of lactic acid right in the muscles. Sort of like litmus paper. When the colour becomes too intense, they should stop automatically. Do you understand what I'm saying? Either they will stop a while of their own accord and rest themselves up, or else someone will inject something to neutralize the acid. If I make that discovery my future is assured. Definitely! International patent, Einstein. Then I can work on the will, George says. That is to say, when I myself have a top management position. Illusions, I say! When did an administrator ever have time for his own research? Look at George: can hardly keep his head above all the papers. So long, bye-bye, Clever. It was nice talking to you.

- I wonder where we're going, he says a little later. I feel rotten. What are we really trying to pull off? What kind of guarantees are there? It's the system, Ypsilon. One cannot be a part of it and remain outside it. Where the hell are we headed, I often wonder. Will we make mankind happier? If not, I have to ask: maybe human happiness never was one of our preliminary assumptions. Maybe we're working against impossible odds. George is more optimistic. He thinks one can improve on the odds. And do away with mankind as a result, I ask? That's a question he doesn't want to answer. Let's take one step at a time, he says. But one step at a time, sooner or later, becomes a mile. But where the hell will we be by then? Sometimes I wonder what you think, Einstein? I do wonder what you think. For Christ's sake, you haven't got anything else to do! Enough to make one jealous. Shall we trade places? You can have a career as a mechanized-monkey mechanic. And I'll sit down in your box with my arms crossed. And *think*. Then I'd be able to solve all the mysteries of

143

the universe. You can use me as a crystal ball. But it mortifies me that the firm, or the cartel, as they say, will get all the credit. In America they have managed to join a frontal lobe and a magnetic memory. Did you know that, Clever? But, of course, there was a rejection reaction. Brain edema. Damned remarkable that you managed to pull through when we put in your antennae. You should have swelled up like a melon. I would like to write a letter to the *Times* about you. I wonder whether what we're doing here isn't an outrage against human rights. You lay in a respirator, wholly cut off from the chin down. Then they got you to sign a paper. Now, how the hell that happened is a question one might very well ask. In any case: they concocted a legally acceptable release. But did you know what you were getting into? No. How could you know that? They didn't know that themselves. I've asked George. He says that the firm has skilful lawyers. We're biologists, not lawyers. Let the lawyers take care of the law. We'd certainly be mad as hell if the attorneys came down here and began to rummage around in our test tubes. George is right about that. No doubt at all. But, still, it feels wrong. When there are a lot of you brains here, I think you ought to form a trade union. One should never rely on specialists. In any case I wouldn't. Everyone has his price. The only question is how much. Well, here I sit, talking my head off. You won't spill the beans now, will you, Einstein?

My eye begins to throb again and he bathes it with an anaesthetic compress. How does he know I'm in pain?

One night while he's working overtime, Curt says:

- Actually, Einstein, you consist of two parts. Your emotional life is concentrated in one half of your brain. In the other is what we call intellect. But we have not yet succeeded in dividing a brain down the middle and getting the two parts to function each on its own. That would be fantastic! I myself wouldn't mind being rid of my emotions. I'd like to have two left halves, two intellect halves. Then my research would be done in a flash.

- Can't you stop chattering and tell me what's become of Flink instead?

144

- Flink?

- The chimpanzee who used to cling to your coattails.

- Not long ago, Flink became ready for greater things, he says sulkily. I don't know if he'll be replaced. Interest in the great apes has declined. Those in the know about such things say nowadays that we humans are closer to the *little* apes. Now they say it's mere superstition that the chimps are our cousins. But Flink sure was entertaining. Good at imitating.

- Is Flink mixed up in your projects for replacing ape-brains with microchips?

- No. Jesus, Ypsilon, you should ask the boss. If my memory hasn't gone completely haywire, Flink has gone over to TV. Some sort of children's programme about Darwin.

- But you operated on him first? Right after his birthday party?

- Don't know. But they didn't send him away straight off. Just as he was, I mean. Flink knew almost everything about us and our work. Always listened in. And of course the industrial secrets had to be erased. Otherwise he could have ended up as prime merchandise on the black market. You have no idea what form industrial espionage takes.

- Are you entirely certain he won't come back?

- I wouldn't count on it, if I were you.

He leaves. I'm left to stew in my own juices. Is it possible that I myself, through my contacts with Flink, have contributed to his banishment? Did they figure out that he stole the case histories? And what shall I do with his memoirs? Cherish them? Why not make them my own? I would gladly swap this place for the Island of the Apes.

42

One night among many: Omega and I lie staring at each other. He still has ears, just as I do. But he seldom uses them. For long periods of time he just lies there, pressing against the bottom of his tank. Is it a 'he'? I think so. Women's ears are generally smaller and rounder, like those of monkeys. Omega's ears are long and limp. Maybe he's old? As one grows older, one's ears become elongated.

I still have not succeeded in making direct contact with Omega. He doesn't respond to signals of any kind. Thought transference doesn't work. For a little while I thought he was defunct. But he is not. During the days he goes through a training programme similar to mine: he watches TV shows - and the psychiatrist sits there with her Rorschach blots in plastic folders.

Tonight the Hand is loose for the first time in ages. It moves around outside Omega's aquarium, fingers the glass, steadies itself on its wrist-stump, and tries to climb up. Sometimes it succeeds in using a sweaty fingertip as a suction cup - only to come tumbling down with its next move. Because Omega is so utterly mute, I focus my attention on the Hand. Soon I have the right feeling; the Hand feels as if it were my own. I guide the Hand inside the hood, to where the oxygen controls and the immersion heater are, and where there's also a little green box - the frequency analyzer. The hand climbs up on the analyzer and from there it proceeds up the immersion heater. When I have it in sight again, it is standing and nosing the lid of Omega's aquarium.

Now Omega reacts: he moves backwards and lowers his rear so

that the finely pleated clump of his cerebellum and the stump of his medulla oblongata become visible. He tries to tip back far enough for the Hand to come within his range of vision; his single eye bobs up and down on the surface like a little buoy. I make the Hand crawl forward so that Omega can see it properly. Then I have the Hand slowly and clearly employ the manual alphabet:

- D-o y-o-u u-n-d-e-r-s-t-a-n-d m-e. G-i-v-e m-e a s-i-g-n . . .

But nothing happens. Omega lies motionless and fixes his gaze on the Hand, like a toad ready to fling out a sticky tongue at a meaty insect. But no attack is launched.

- M-y n-a-m-e i-s Y-p-s-i-l-o-n. Y-o-u-r n-a-m-e i-s O-m-e-g-a.

No reply. But we've got plenty of time. Maybe we'll lie here in our isolation cells for years and years. We'll have ages to devise our own prison code, one we can tap along the pipes.

Suddenly the Hand is down on the frequency analyzer again, without my having commanded it. I give the order, 'stop'; but the Hand does not stop. It is already climbing on the parrakeet cage. I give up. I've never been one hundred per cent successful in directing the Hand. Let it do as it likes! Omega is still lying in the same absurd, backward-tipped position. To hell with them, I say, placing myself instead at the bottom of my tank, where I press the globe of my eye against the glass to sleep a while.

I'm brutally awakened by the Hand hanging on to the upper rim of my aquarium by its fingertips. He hangs there and time after time bangs his wrist against the glass, so that a boom resonates through the water. What's the matter with that idiot?! I swim backwards and stare up at the Hand.

- You are my Hand! Obey me!

I have no control whatsoever over the Hand. It climbs around the four sides of the aquarium, hanging by its fingertips. All the way along it swings the rump of its wrist and pounds it against the glass. I try to follow all its sweeps and turns, to keep it before my eye the whole time. My ears beat in a frenzy. I become nervous and conduct myself like an inexperienced oarsman. Without knowing how it has happened, I am lying in a supine position.

I no longer have eye contact with the Hand. But I can feel that it is now up on top of my aquarium. It is jumping up and down; the stamping goes through the water like shock waves. I feel sick. The pounding simply continues. It is as if they had placed a big, living heart right next to me. When the heart beats I lose both sight and sensation. Between beats I see glimpses of the laboratory. Omega no longer lies staring upward. Instead he is standing as far forward in his tank as possible, fixing his burning eye upon me.

I don't regain consciousness until it is time for the morning rounds. The professor, the psychiatrist, and Curt crouch around and stare. Then the professor carefully rights me. Anxious, they look at me. The psychiatrist walks away and borrows Omega's EEG-machine.

- Lidocaine drops! says the professor, and Curt fetches a flask and transfer pipette assembly from the refrigerator.

They drop the solution into the water. I ache all over and feel dizzy. The psychiatrist connects me to the electro-encephalograph. The roll of graph paper in the machine starts to move. They lift up the broad strip of paper and scrutinize it. The professor outlines the curve with a red marking pen. Quickly they nod to one another.

- Ypsilon, says the professor. We believe you have had an epileptic seizure. We don't know if this is an isolated occurrence. We don't know what's triggered it. You will have to stay on lidocaine a while yet, for safety's sake. I also want you to pay particular heed to any changes that may take place in you. I want you to be especially attentive to strange spots of light, peeping or screeching sounds, peculiar odours, or if you feel strange in general. Such things can presage another seizure. This is called an aura. But above all, you shouldn't fret about it. If you've got a touch of epilepsy, it's not the end of the world. We can hold it in check. By the way, did you know that epilepsy formerly was called 'the sacred disease'? That's no joke - almost something to be proud of!

I want to scream out after them: I am something big, something unprecedented! Despite the fact that at first I was nothing at all, a single cell. With time a neural tube, an embryo, a thinking pinhead that grew into the sleek, innocent brain of the foetus. Then the ethereal brain of a small child, the confused brain of a schoolboy, the worried and wrinkled brain of a teenager, and now: the consummate thinking machine, tamed and domesticated like an atomic reactor. But for God's sake, look out for the day when the emergency cooling system breaks down!

I am very tired. I cannot bear to move my bruised flesh. Once they've vanished, I lie listlessly and glare at Emma, who is reading aloud to Omega. He stares over her shoulder. That same, obstinately glaring snake's eye.

43

How lovely it is to be convalescent! But it also invites brooding. I cannot forget Flink. Now that he's gone, he takes on entirely different proportions. In my imagination he is bigger, more dignified, yes, even severe. I feel like a child compared to him. I know he will never come back. While Flink was 'still alive', if someone had told me that I would mourn him, I would have laughed. He was an insufferable chatterbox, completely devoid of charm.

What shall I do with Flink's childhood isle, the Island of the Apes? It is mine now. He'll never come climbing up here, demanding to have it returned. The more I think about the Island of the Apes, the more it becomes my own. It is no longer Flink's childhood, but mine. The Island of the Apes lives on in me. In the hothouse of my brain it grows and flourishes. At first I tried to sort out the individuals who live there. I was curious as to whether they were chimps - or human beings. But I'll never succeed in getting a firm fix on them. Nor does it matter. Once mature, who cares any longer about how his parents look? In childhood, one is extremely concerned that one's parents do not differ from those of other children; they shouldn't be any older, have less money, a different outlook on life, or wear strange clothes. But for me as an adult, relationships are the crucial things.

I sit at the water's edge and poke in the sand with a dry stick. I am waiting for Mother. She has gone to fetch the day's food ration from the metal container where each daily allotment is doled out automatically. I'm not allowed to go there with her. They don't want kids hanging and climbing around there. I haven't seen my father at all today. As usual, he is trying to see justice is done in a long, drawn-out dispute. It's a matter of right of possession of a tree that washed ashore. One morning last summer the tree was lying on our little stretch of beach. We just let it lie there - 'mañana' is always the prevalent attitude here. But the next night a storm suddenly blew up, and the tree was driven out by the waves, and some days later it was washed up a few beach-lots farther down. Those who lived there now consider the tree theirs. Father and his brothers went down there to take the tree home. But they were driven away. Now the grown men of the clan sit assembled on a big sunny rock, chewing peapods and pursuing litigation. While Mother fetches food.

I am not an entirely happy child. I often sit by myself and scratch signs in the sand. They have no meaning. I just sit and draw the same patterns over and over again. I don't know what this means, but it makes me feel calmer. Sometimes I fantasize that a huge catastrophe takes place. That a forest fire destroys our scraggly pines and scrubby, dry juniper bushes. Or that a huge deluge comes and sweeps us all out into the grey sea. I would like to draw up a list of those who should drown - and those who will be allowed to survive. But I cannot write. When I get up to six or seven names, I lose the thread and have to start all over again from the beginning. Why doesn't Mother come? If Mother doesn't come before the sun has passed the trunk of the big oak tree, I will include her in the list of those who shall die.

My friends are nowhere to be seen. To hell with them. We hardly ever have any fun. Just hang around in the trees and loaf about. Or sit on some stones on the beach and smear them all over with spit that we rub round and round again with our index fingers. I want us kids to build something. But I never get to decide what we do. Even when we agree that I'll be the one to decide, it never turns out that way in the end. What's character-istic of the kids around here is that they never keep their word!

Every autumn and spring the Selection Committee comes here.

Then we all devoutly assemble ourselves into families. I have two elder brothers who have been selected. Exactly what for I don't know. First everybody goes to some sort of camping school, of course. It's a huge disgrace not to be chosen. You should either get married and start a family of your own or else be selected. Otherwise you have no dignity. Then all you can do for the rest of your life is loaf. If you are male, you are forbidden to join in on the lawsuits on the sunny rock. If you are female, you can only get food after all the married women have taken theirs.

Now the sun has passed the oak. I raise the penalty for Mother. If she doesn't come before the sun has reached the old crow's nest in the tree next to it, I will think up something even more devilish. We should dig out a deep pit and shove her into it. Then we'd all piss and shit in the hole. It will have drainage, so she won't drown. But up to her neck she shall stand. We'll give her a little food and water; killing her is not part of the plan.

Now the sun has gone by the crow's nest. We must come up with something still worse. Sometimes a few of us are taken away for medical experimentation. But that happens very seldom. Only the incredibly stupid are caught for that purpose. But they take only those who are physically healthy. They don't take invalids or cripples. That's why there aren't very many of them. It seems that if one is not right in the head, one is almost always physically weak too. But we ought to be able to force Mother to volunteer. We could trick her: tell her she's taking the boat to go and visit my two brothers. She ought to go along with that. She's always longing to see them - to my great annoyance. After all, I'm the littlest! I'm the one who needs her most. If Mother doesn't come before the sun has reached the surveillance bunker on the rocky islet just across the sound, we will steal some kerosene and pour it over her. Then it's only a matter of summoning up a match. But that shouldn't be very difficult. When the Selection Committee comes, they never pay much attention to their things. We children usually go through their packs or steal right out of their pockets. Stuffed down in an old woodpecker's hole, I've got a broken pipe and five bottle openers.

Now Mother is coming! With my nose hot and clogged with tears, I rush towards her and throw myself into her arms, with such speed that she drops the basket of corncobs. Furious, she strips me off her; I land on my rump in a little pool on the beach.

44

Emma, why are you forsaking me? All I see is your back, the nape of your neck, your calves that stretch when you stand on your toes to reach the panel of fuses above Omega's aquarium. Now and then I have the pleasure of seeing you in profile, when you take the Hand in your lap to give it its daily nutrient injection. Never a glance, never a friendly word in passing. When you sit way over there and read aloud from the sports equipment catalogue - why must you hold your cupped hand in front of the corner of your mouth? You know I can hear you anyway! You know that I know all the pages by heart. By the way, whatever happened to 'Fjellsikker', the Norwegian anorak I asked you to send for?

Hastily she turns her head and glowers at me - only to pretend a moment later that I've never existed.

Is something wrong, Emma? You could confide in me. You've listened to my problems, now I'm ready to listen to yours. After all, that's the basis for all interpersonal relationships: trust. I realize that Omega has a greater claim on your time than I do. After all, he's new here. But surely he doesn't need every single, god-damned second! I don't want to speak disparagingly of Omega, but I'm not one hundred per cent convinced that he wishes you well. Or me. What do we know about his background? If I were in your shoes, I would go down to the basement and take his records out of the locked filing cabinet. No, I don't want to know about him. I want you to know. Why shouldn't we take each other's backgrounds into consideration - we almost always do that in normal circumstances. We rarely allow other human beings to get close to us without knowing something about where they come from, what they do professionally, what they're interested in . . . Call it bourgeois if you like! I believe that it's universal.

- Stop it! she suddenly screams across the laboratory.

No, I have no intention of stopping. Do you know why: because I have nothing to lose. I have clung to your skirts, like a lovesick boy, long enough. Put up with all sorts of whimsical behaviour. Always tried to look happy. All the while I've been afraid of seeming insipid - but I haven't dared utter a word of criticism. I have turned myself inside out. I have tackled every task you have deigned to confer upon me with superhuman efforts. And I've done all this only to avoid hearing you say that you don't love me.

It can't go on like this. We cannot go on being hypocritical indefinitely. I am not demanding that you tell me you love me. Who can *demand* such a thing? Until now I believed that I needed to be allowed to hope in order to go on living. But let's take the bull by the horns: I will go on in any case. After all, I'm not the one who decides the matter. Even if I were still a whole human being, in full possession of arms and legs, it would be unlikely that I could decide whether to end my own life. In spite of everything, few people take their own lives. I could never bring myself . . . I imagine that it happens in a kind of trance, in the narrow vacuum between happiness and despair. Could you, Emma, would you be able to . . .

- If you don't shut up, we'll go out into the utility room to read!

Go ahead. Go ahead and take your companion, or your companions out with you to the utility room. Surely the Hand is listening too? What does he want from the catalogue? A pigskin glove from Taiwan, 'Pimpernel' style? For Omega I think you should knit a cap, like the egg-warmer you made for Flink. Do you remember Flink, Emma? Excuse me. I'm not myself. Yes I am, Emma: I am myself. This is how I *am*. When I'm not, at any price, shamming in order to please someone else. Of course, this is somewhat more than the real me - I'm loaded, ready to explode. I've bottled up so much inside me these last few months. If I am unusually nice and docile tomorrow, don't take that as a sign of my normal condition. I am just as self-centred, just as uncertain, just as much in need of laying my head in your lap as all the other men you have met.

- Now I am going! Emma says. She stuffs the catalogue into her coat pocket, folds up the chair with a bang, looks at the clock on the wall, and leaves the laboratory.

Go sit in the staff room, then. Sit there and smoke and stare at the coffee urn; it still has a long way to go before the water boils. Sit there way in advance of all the others. If you're thinking of crying, by the way, you'd better go to the bathroom. Just bear in mind that it takes three quarters of an hour before you can show your face again without anyone asking you any questions. You can hear me just as well in the staff room as in here. I can even reach you in the animal department up in the attic. Or in the secretary's office. All the way down in Curt's room, you will hear me more faintly. If you want to be absolutely sure of escaping me, you will have to go home.

What's your place like, Emma? You have a balcony - I know that from the time when we could still talk to each other. You have a cat named Mozart, a castrated jade who never goes out of doors. Not even on to the balcony, because he's afraid of seagulls. Come to think of it, who took care of him - it? - when you went on vacation? Your mother? You've become such good friends since you moved away from home. Absence makes the heart grow fonder, so the saying goes. Are you satisfied with your life? Or better: are you thinking of doing anything about it?

Now I can hear you punching out your timecard - on the line that reads menstrual pains or the one for migraine? Pardon me, Emma, although you cannot hear me any longer. Why have things come to such a pass between us? It's not natural. After all, to you I'm only a pet. Not so naively devoted as a dog; nor can I get myself into the studiedly indolent positions that Mozart does. I have to just lie here. If I haven't had an epileptic fit, of course.

Forgive me! I believe I understand what is going on: you have had your orders. George and the research team have taken you aside, leafed through my programme, and said: Well, Emma, we think you ought to keep Ypsilon on tenterhooks a while longer. We suspect that too much friendliness engages his neurons. You distract him. That is not a criticism, rather it's a compliment. You know how highly we all value your contribution to the project. You are dependable, discerning, and quick on the uptake. Unfortunately, it seems Ypsilon thinks so too. That's why he cannot help becoming attached. If something out of the ordinary happens, we count on your reporting it in due course. That's how it is, isn't it, Emma?!

45

All through the nights Omega and Ypsilon lie, staring fixedly at each other. Yes, I'm beginning to speak baby talk and refer to myself in the third person. How can one possibly be adult here? Who has lain in an incubator longer than I? Ypsilon, the incredible infant phenomenon at just over a kilo.

The Hand is sleeping, curled up with its fist half-closed. No one sleeps with his hand open flat; no one wants to awaken with a glob of green slime someone has coughed up, or an egg covered with scales that the devil's left in his palm, between the life line and the line of fate. I don't dare do anything with the Hand any longer. I fancy that as long as I leave off guiding the Hand around, Omega will also let it alone. A silent agreement. But maybe, too, a first step towards contact. Our relationship is no longer entirely mute, we seem to have adopted a wait-and-see policy.

Life on the Island of Apes goes on much as usual. I have grown no older since last time. My contacts with others have not become more open or more natural. Papa goes on sitting and carrying on his lawsuit on the sunny rock. When she goes to fetch food and water, Mamma is gone for hours. In the evenings we all sit around the fire and the elders reel off their eternal, repetitive memories of life in the jungle. If one sneaks forward and pokes in the fire with a stick, one can count on having one's ears boxed.

Does Omega also have his own Island of the Apes? Or has he grown up among flying foxes in a dank and mouldy cave? My grandfather has died. When someone dies on the Island of the

Apes, he is buried in the sand in a sitting position with his face towards Africa. He died a long time ago - why should I bother myself about it? When my great-grandfather died I wasn't even born. I don't want to know about the thousands of old men who stand on my shoulders, a rickety pillar that disappears way up above the clouds. Old men who claim to be my forefathers and therefore demand mourning and respect. What is the Island of the Apes? Nothing but a stale filled doughnut, a dreary, half-civilized life. Without the state, we wouldn't make it through a single winter. We're no good at fishing. If we grub for roots, we invite our own ruin. In a few years' time we will have transformed our scrubby, sandy isle into a barren rock polished clean.

I pace out my living space. The tank is five brain-lengths long, three wide, and four high. Elbow room, nothing more. If I turn too sharply, my own cerebral nerves - which usually trail below me - can land on top, like hair over my eye. This can injure my eye, since I can't blink the strands away.

Like a flatfish I press myself against the bottom, turn my back on the harsh light of the lab, and squeeze myself down below the tube that continually releases oxygen. It is delightful when I manage to get the roly-poly bubbles to tickle my crevices and folds. I lie there staring into the hood's dusky, tiled inside. Maybe when George is through with me, I can get a job as a watchman. Like a mini-submarine or a sailing TV camera I could crisscross the navy yards and docks, scrutinizing every inch and reporting on the slightest deviation. All that I need is a lightweight but powerful miner's helmet for the greater depths. Would I be able to survive the cold? What happens when the ice starts to set? Will I be able to rely on my sense of direction, or will they have to set up a small radio-beacon on one of the docks 24 hours a day, so that I don't go astray under the ice and get frozen fast?

If I didn't have to stay in the water, by now I could have been going at top speed and risen up out of the aquarium like a hovercraft and moved about freely in the room. I don't know how I'll get out of the laboratory. All the doors are sure to be locked; there's a lot of expensive equipment here - as well as alcohol, chemicals, and other desirable items. On top of that there's the security camera. If I tried to get through the ventilation system, a fan blade would slice me up. But if someone were to leave a window open! Like a plump flying saucer I could sail out over the park in the moonlight. Where would I go? It's not exactly as if there were someone sitting and waiting for me with coffee on the stove.

I would like to meet God. God is in heaven; it is only in the beginning of the Old Testament that he finds himself on earth. In the 19th century, barely nine billion years after creation, God sent Charles Darwin to the South Seas to take stock of the evolutionary situation of the day - will it be another nine billion years before the next general inventory?

What will Darwin find then? Nine billion years from now? Next time he comes here and tries to take the first available ship to his beloved Galapagos Islands - how will the finches look then? In accordance with the law of the survival of the fittest, in all those billions of years, every living creature ought to have taken a giant step forward. All one has to do is look back and compare. Where are they now, the giant lizards, the flying snakes, the unicorns, the sabre-toothed tiger, the Neanderthal Man? I believe I am a pioneer. In the future the whole earth will be covered by water. All the mammals, birds, and insects will live together in one gigantic pool - if the sun continues to shine, *nota bene*; otherwise we will all lie frozen solid, as in an abandoned supermarket freezer.

When Darwin Number Two, Darwin's Son, or whatever he-she-it may be called, returns to the earth - to what will be nothing but a tepid, slightly saline sea - how will the flora and fauna look then? By that time, all the species of animals will have left their bodies behind them. They will be simpler and less vulnerable. Blood, bone, marrow, liver, heart, and kidneys - all emblematic of vulnerability - will disappear. No one will lug around long legs, sprawling feathers, sore fins, chipped horns, or scales blackened by vitamin deficiencies. In the warm sea everyone will live in harmony. Each species and family will pretty much stick together, but without struggles or wars with their environment. All that will remain of us will be our brains, with an eye and two outer ears, of course. We need to swim not so that we can hunt, but so that we're mobile enough not to get stuck eternally in the same rock crevice. When one goes out for a spin, one will meet whale or elephant brains, which, when asleep, press into one another like huge pillows. Small finch brains that flit about. Dolphin brains that slide through the waves in sleek arcs. A shark brain or two with fine stunted fins drooping on their crowns. Nobody will eat anybody else. The ocean itself will be full of sugars and salts that we'll absorb through the cerebellum's gills.

46

- How are things going in the brainwashing department today?
Curt asks and takes a pinch of snuff.

I don't answer. I've learned that he doesn't expect me to. He
makes jokes to cheer himself up when he's feeling insecure. He
has taped a big wiring diagram to the wall. With his mouth half-
open and a bulging upper lip, he stares at his map. On the back
of a telephone message pad he makes his own rough sketch and
orientates himself. Once his preparations are done, he goes
searching through the room for a fuse, a connection, or a relay.
But the wiring diagram portrays an idealized picture of reality.
Several times he's on the verge of giving up.

- I'm doing this for you, Ypsilon. I thought you ought to get
out and about a bit.

He goes around the room with his little slip of paper as if on a
treasure hunt. They've made so many changes here in the lab that
by now the electrical system is nothing but a kitchen midden.
When he's finally found the connection box he's been looking
for - under the window seat - he swears aloud for joy. He
unscrews it and brings it over so I can see it: 24 fuses that look
like small whistles, clogged with sticky dustballs and strands of
hair.

- Damned lucky that your skull hasn't shorted out.

He puts a number on the wiring diagram and writes the same
number on a piece of marking tape, which he pastes on to the lid
of the fusebox. Then, without cleaning it off, he screws the box
back in place.

- Humpty Dumpty sat on a wall. Humpty Dumpty had a great fall. All the king's horses and all the king's men, couldn't put Humpty together again! Curt chants to himself, and points a Phillips screwdriver towards the TV camera. I thought we should make a little, unscheduled experiment. Your right Nervus Opticus is free in any case.

He means that I still have a blindly projecting optic nerve from my other, amputated eye. Until now I had not understood why they had removed one of my eyes but left its nerve stem. But I'm beginning to get an idea.

- As easy as pie, no more difficult than connecting a TV to an aerial, Curt says.

He takes a rolled-up TV cable from his pocket, and tears open its sturdy plastic packaging with his teeth. On either end of the white cord is a small metal cap.

- This ought to work, he says, scrutinizing the opening of the cap. Your optic nerve is indeed a bit narrower than the cable, but if you can hold still, I think it will stay on.

He gets a stool, puts it under the security camera, and climbs up. He disconnects the camera from its ordinary circuit - which carries its images to a surveillance centre somewhere or other - and clips in the TV cable he has brought with him in its place. Carefully he climbs down and lays out the cord behind him on the floor as he approaches me. Before he goes any further, he takes a fresh pinch of snuff.

- It's a matter of remaining clearheaded, Ypsilon . . . Now, unfortunately, I'll have to turn you upside down in order to thread the cable on to your optic nerve.

He turns me belly up in a calm and careful way that one generally does not associate with his efforts. When he slides the metal cap over my optic nerve, I don't feel a thing. Then he turns me right side up again.

- Are you ready now, Einstein?

The camera image hits me with a shock, as when one shines a strong lamp on to the eyelids of a sleeping person. The whole inside of my head turns a pale red. Sight in my eye vanishes;

everything sparkles a blinding white.
- Don't make me snowblind!!
- I'll turn it down a little.

The sparkling white goes over into grey. Some minutes later I have regained sight in my own eye: Omega lies and glares as usual, without the slightest change of expression. In my other, hooked-up eye, a blurry image flickers in white and grey. Slowly it becomes more distinct. Its gaze sweeps over the laboratory. I see a light, tiled floor and four high windows with drawn blinds. To the left, a wide hood piled up with aquariums - when the camera moves toward the right, I see a man in an unbuttoned white coat extending two fingers towards me in a V-sign. Behind him there's a smaller hood with a single aquarium. I don't see myself, owing to reflections in the water.

- Hold a black disc in front of my real eye!
- No need to. You'll adjust soon enough. It's like looking into a microscope. Only beginners hold something in front of or squint up the free eye. One soon learns to concentrate on only one eye.

He's right. After a few more sweeps over the lab, the colour image of Omega pales away, while the camera-eye image becomes all the more distinct. It is still black and white, but sharp, with the exception of a grey band that moves from top to bottom every few seconds.

- Pull up the blinds!
The figure down there on the tiled floor shuffles off to the window seat and pulls a few cords. He's only entirely successful with one of them; in the other three windows the venetian blinds hang rather lopsidedly. Outside the window is a car park. It is crammed full. Cars are parked halfway on the grassy spots, or partially block off the adjacent streets. Beyond the car park stands a light-coloured highrise block. On its facade is a large neon sign: BIOCHINE. Beneath the sign is a dark square, on which temperature and time flash alternately. Right now it is 17:03 and +6.

Suddenly it strikes me! I *am* up here in the camera. This is where I *exist*. My sense of location in the brain has disappeared!

164

It is true that every time the camera turns right, I am looking at the aquarium - but it means nothing to me. It could just as well be someone else who is lying down there. Well, it's an old observation: man is in his senses. But there's a big difference. Ordinarily our senses - eyes, ears, nose - are plastered on to our brains. Now the distance is something like ten metres as the crow flies. This gives me an enormous, an overwhelming sense of freedom.

   - Let me stay here!

   - You are mad, Ypsilon. I have to take you down again. You can't just sit under the rafters forever and lay eggs like a bird that's escaped from its cage.

47

In the middle of the night I am awakened by nails scraping on the glass. The anti-epileptic drops often make me vacillate between sleeping and waking states nowadays. The Hand stands propped against the short end of the tank, its fingers extended like claws. I cower. I hope they've doped me up with enough medicine, in case the Hand climbs in here to short-circuit me.

After my initial flight reaction, I try to gain control over the Hand. It doesn't work. I know that I can't affect the Hand's movements unless I can simultaneously receive its sensory impressions, that is to say, pressure against the fingertips or muscular movements. I feel nothing. But the Hand's still clinging to my glass tank. Straight across the room Omega rests with his eternally glaring eye. But the Hand makes no attempt to climb up. It moves back and stands poised at the edge of the hood, resting on its thumb and little finger, supported on the back of its wrist. Its index finger, middle finger, and ring finger grope in the air. It is trying to say something. I have difficulty reading it. A sign language that employs only three fingers is like a typewriter missing some of its keys.

- O-M G-A . . .

Omega? Is Omega finally trying to break his silence? Immediately I'm prepared to sign back with my own name - with what shall I sign? I drift toward the bottom and lie there pressing heavily against my own eye, so that the images are twisted and distorted. The Hand is transformed into a flabby octopus with long, billowing, snaky fingers. I pull myself together, rise up, and concentrate

on the Hand.
- O-M G-A S-C R-D, it says.
Omega scared? I focus my thoughts into a telepathic answer:
- Answer if you hear me! Answer 'yes' if you hear me! The Hand's fingers sink down towards the tiled bottom of the hood. Then it laboriously raises its ring finger in the air and signs:
- S.
Yes? I take a new initiative through thought transference.
- How much is four times four?
- S X-T-E.
There is no longer any doubt that contact has been established. Omega hears me well. However, Omega's aptitude for expressing himself is severely impaired.
- Do not be afraid. One survives, look at me!
- B-R-D, the Hand answers.
Bored? What the hell else do you expect! I get irritated, as if *I* haven't been bored here?! One must bear in mind that until now I have been *alone*. That is if one disregards the dog, Flink, and the staff - and the Hand, which doesn't really count. Nor did I have the benefit of going through orientation here in the lab with an older brain.
- You will have to get used to it. That's what I had to do.
- T-L L.
Tell? What does Omega want me to tell him - a bedtime story? I feel like an idiot lying here and telling stories to a . . . machine? Is Omega a machine? He can count and make monosyllabic statements. But in what shape is the emotional life over there on the other side of the lab? Is there really any reason to believe that Omega ought to be any more stupid than I am? It hardly seems likely. When I first came here, the staff treated me like an infant just learning to walk. Despite the fact that my intelligence quotient was sky-high above theirs. The thought suddenly strikes me that maybe Omega is superior to me. Maybe he's speaking baby talk so as not to disconcert me. I don't want Omega to have a higher IQ. The thought of submitting to him scares me more than the thought of being subject to the pro-

fessor. Why? Is it harder for us to yield to our own kind?

- I will tell you about the Island of the Apes, I say.

- A-P I-S-L-D! the Hand signs, full of expectation.

- Once upon a time there was a chimpanzee named Flink. He lived here in the laboratory. With time, he became a friend of the staff and got to make the rounds with them. They all thought he went along so he wouldn't be bored and so he could meet people. But that wasn't the whole truth: Flink was looking for an ally, someone who would listen to the story of his life. You see, Flink was no ordinary laboratory ape. He had grown up in freedom, or out of doors in any case. He came from a place called the Island of the Apes. I don't know where it is, but to judge from scattered bits of information, it's in an archipelago, or possibly in a large lake. There, on a little island with rounded rocks, scrubby young saplings, a few evergreens and leafy trees together with a bit of flat sandy beach, Flink grew up with his mamma and papa.

- M-A M-A N-D A-P.

- Yes, mamma and papa. Later, when Flink got bigger and it became evident that he was among the more gifted children of his age, he got to leave the Island of the Apes and go to school. Do you know what happened to the Island of the Apes then? One night a violent storm came and flooded the whole island. Many drowned, but a few of them clung tightly to some worn-out dog kennels and windfallen trees and managed to paddle themselves over to the mainland. The island itself, however, was torn loose from the bedrock and drifted off out to sea. It drifted for months and years, finally it landed at the bottom of the sea, several kilometres below the surface. That was in one of the warm oceans. That's where the old Island of the Apes came to rest. Deep-sea fishes and molluscs investigated the sunken isle, but none of them dared to settle there. It looked more like a shipwreck than anything else - and the creatures of the sea had learned to avoid wrecks. Wrecks often were filled with poisons and oil that leaked out when the tanks rusted. That's why the island just lay there uninhabited until one day two peculiar creatures came swimming through the depths. They were as alike as two peas in a pod. But these weren't just any ordinary peas. They were almost as large as ostrich eggs and they came trailing long filaments, like jellyfish. These creatures knew that the Island of the Apes was not dangerous. That's why they could settle down there, each in his own rock-crevice, only a few metres away from each other. And do you know what the two companions were called? They were called Ypsilon and . . .

- O-M G-A.

- Their names were Ypsilon and Omega. And do you know who they had with them, who was their friend and protector, but who didn't resemble them at all, but looked like a mermaid? She wasn't exactly dressed in gold lamé and she didn't have a tail like a fish. Instead, she had a diver's mask on her face, an oxygen tank on her back, and flippers on her feet. Her name was . . .

- E M-A!

- Her name was Emma, and she was Omega's and Ypsilon's best friend. Now I think it's time you went to sleep. Are you feeling calmer now?

- G-D N-I T.

Now there are two of us brains here. Perhaps one shouldn't get one's hopes up too high concerning Omega, but one can state a simple fact: we are *two*. Only now can I openly admit my misgivings. I had thought of Omega as my successor. I believed that Biochine considered me a failure. As soon as they'd seen that Omega had made progress, they would get rid of me. For what else could have become of Alpha, Beta, Gamma, and so forth? The whole series of brains who have lain here, sweating - how long ago? Years? Decades?

Tomorrow night I will begin to talk seriously with Omega. There are two things we have to do: stick together but at the same time still cooperate with our employers. Using our talent, we have to make them respect us. They won't do anything to us as long as they need us. And we will *gladly* cooperate. If we just lie here and do only what is absolutely necessary, it won't do anyone any good. On the contrary, we will take them by storm. After all, there is nothing that says it's we who will submit ourselves in the long run. We can become the masters here. Even if we're sort of dependent on our caretakers, still, we can be the ones to make the decisions. Man's conquest of all other species of animals on the earth depends, after all, on his superior intelligence. But his mastery will last only as long as he can maintain his lead. As a species, Omega and I are superior to humankind.

48

Curt comes trotting along into the laboratory a good while before it is time for the morning rounds. He pulls up a stool and sits down with his elbow in the hood and leans his forehead against the edge. It can be seen a mile away that he has been up all night.

- Today I must say goodbye, Ypsilon. My appointment terminates at the end of the month. But I'm going home now.

- Does that mean that Emma will take care of me?

- But before I go, I mean to tell you some of the facts. It pains me to see you lying here like an idiot! Do you know why they're giving me the boot? Because you and I fooled around with the security camera. And they didn't even discover it until yesterday! No one has time to go through all the video cassettes. But yesterday the police were here in connection with the disappearance of a number of case histories. So they sat down and looked through all the cassettes. And what do they discover? Well now, there's a break in the film. And before the break comes, they see me preparing to splice in some wires. But that's not it, Ypsilon! That's only a pretext. And that's what makes me so damned furious! Who gets fired for a little experimental zeal? No, it's because of my research. They think it's going too slowly. They don't understand that serious research takes time. Not even George grasps it. Maybe he does, deep down. But, after all, he's got the accountants breathing down his neck.

- That's really a shame.

- But they can't put a muzzle on me. Not inside here at any

rate. On the outside I can't say a word without getting caught. But you're not an industrial spy. In any event, not in the technical, the legal sense of the word. On the contrary, you're an idiot. You and your friend, Omega; you who should be so damned intelligent. You don't understand a thing! You think you are some kind of goddam mascot here, eh? But you're only one experimental animal among many. What have we been doing these last months? Guess! No, you'll never guess. We have been waiting for your emotional life to collect itself where it belongs, in the right half of your brain. Do you see? We're sifting the wheat from the chaff. Emotions to the right, wits to the left . . .

He titters a little at his witticism, looks up at the clock, and using an old, disposable syringe with no needle, plugs a pinch of snuff under his lip.

- Promise me one thing, Ypsilon! Never begin to take snuff.
- Why do I have to have my emotions on the right?
- You know that as well as I do: as long as everything is one big tangle inside your skull, they can't very well isolate your various functions. The day they succeed in dividing you up into different pieces, umm, that's when you'll really be useful as hell . . . Your output will be cleaner, they'll just take out what they want. What they don't want they can just shut off or dispose of. 'Washed intelligence', George said at the meeting on Friday. But we said the term sounded too loaded. Scrap 'washed'. The word has definite drawbacks. 'Directed' was the term we suggested. But George didn't think that was any better. Now the whole language department is working on it. If one has experts, one must make use of them, of course.
- So, a whole lot of what I've been forced to experience here, on the emotional level, has been so that my feelings would assemble themselves . . .
- *Everything*. Never, ever believe that anything that happens here happens by chance. Except for my sitting here and babbling my head off, of course. That's not part of the programme.
- What a relief!
- A relief? How so? Are you happy to hear that you are a

marionette, pure and simple?!

- It's about Emma. You know that Emma does nothing but turn her back on me nowadays. If I understand you right, that, too, is part of the programme? Actually, I've figured that out by myself.

- Emma? Should she be part of the programme?

- Everything, that's what you just said.

- Emma is a problem all by herself, Ypsilon. But I'll tell you this as one man to another: we had a brief affair, she and I. And maybe you didn't know this, but, after all, I have a wife and kids. Not good, not good at all. She got pregnant, you see. And had to get rid of it. Much weeping and gnashing of teeth beforehand; but, after all, it was the only sensible thing to do. Even if one has to take the blame and come off like a shit. Sometimes one has to play the bad guy for other people's best interest. A simple D&C. But, unfortunately, not entirely free of complications, as it turned out. Here at work she said she'd been to Mallorca. She borrowed my sun lamp.

- But if it's not part of the programme, then what reason does she have to turn her back on me?!

- Be a little cool, now: what reason has she got *not* to turn her back on you? You and your buddy here, I know you both practise your charm on the female personnel. But seriously? You think she likes you? I know that sometimes she has to go out to the locker room and puke. She thinks you are both repulsive. It took a long time, all the way down to the one we called Sigma, before Emma learned to handle a living brain.

- But my name is Ypsilon. The one lying over there, why is his name Omega? There ought to be three others between us: Phi, Chi, and Psi.

- In between? Umhum. No, they were duds, as we say. Never began to function. The technique is still in its infancy. The two of you here, if not unique in the world, are pretty nearly so. The round will be coming soon, now. I want to say something about the future here . . .

- Let's go over this business with Emma one more time!

- Honestly speaking, I find it awkward.

- Can you *swear* that Emma did not get orders to turn her back on me?!

- Sure, I swear.

- How then can you explain that she actually held me in her lap, that she read to me, that she - whether or not you believe it - kissed this very glass!

- Well, what do you think? Of course all *that* was part of the programme. So that all of Ypsilon's feelings would surface and be gathered in the correct place, somebody had to stimulate him . . . I have heard George say so myself. But now even you yourself can see: look at her sitting there, having a fine old time with Omega. Your course of treatment is over as far as she is concerned. Now she can show you what she *really* thinks of you . . .

- Good morning boys!

It is the research team with the professor in the lead. He lays a heavy hand on Curt's lowered head. Without so much as tossing me a parting glance, Curt ducks under George's arm and slinks out of the room.

- He came to say goodbye, I say.

- Curt has a new assignment, George says. But you, Ypsilon, you are making fine progress. Beyond our expectations. We are very satisfied with you. I think you ought to know that. I'm not one to squander words of praise. But if there's really good reason for praise, then it should be conveyed; that has always been my policy.

174

49

I have made up my mind to attempt to escape from here. I cannot lie here any longer among my fantasies and wild hopes for a more dignified life. Practically speaking, a successful escape is almost unthinkable. But what have I got to lose? My only alternative is suicide. Thus, I have nothing to lose. But I haven't the slightest idea about how to carry it off; not a single clue. So I lie around, envying the classical fugitives: Casanova slinking out of the 'Leads' in the Doge's Palace, or the Count of Monte Cristo sewing himself into a sack for corpses and getting himself thrown into the sea. Child's play. My escape lacks precedents. A patient who picks himself up from the operating table - with sheets and tubes, clamps and sutures swinging around his body - and bounds out of the room, pushing the respirator before him like a baby carriage: if only my chances were as good as his!

If I do not succeed I will take my own life. It seems reasonable to begin from there, with the second alternative. If the escape fails, I cannot *then* count on having the requisite concentration to plan a suicide. There have been unusual suicides: a Roman slave is said to have taken his life by stopping breathing; but in modern times that method has not shown itself to be feasible. Among certain primitive peoples, it is said that sometimes someone decides to die - and then wastes away. Can I rely on such a method? How long will it take? Won't the instruments betray me before then? How is it possible for me to die - I who have a theoretical life span of 800 years?

I must have assistance. Who will help me? I hardly think the staff would. If I die, the lab's funding may be endangered. The staff could be threatened with transfer. I cannot count on voluntary help. Maybe I could trick someone into doing something capricious, so that I get dropped on the tiled floor. Will I die then? After all, I'm not an egg, but a soft, rather plastic mass laced through with threads and stays, like the tough clay between the roots of a tree. Maybe they'll just laugh at me, pick me up, rinse me off, and stick me back in the aquarium.

If the environment here in the aquarium changes, I will die. It may take time, but I will not survive a pronounced increase or decrease in temperature. Nor will I survive a change in the chemical composition of the solution. If the oxygen pump stops working for long periods of time, I would die then, too. But here two main problems arise: for one thing, someone has to turn off the oxygen pump, for example. And for the other, the shut-off must not trigger an alarm or an automatic transfer to the reserve pump. Nonetheless, on rare occasions the surveillance system is turned off for shorter or longer intervals. For example, when they made renovations here and laid down new cables and pipes. How long will it be before they make further changes?

One thing is clear: while I am planning, I must, whatever the price, get the research team to believe that I'm cooperating. My starting position isn't bad. After all, I've just been praised for my progress. Maybe it would have been better if the progress had come somewhat later, which is to say, after I'd begun to plan for my escape or death. But really, the solution is not so bad. No one can reasonably suspect my plans. Unless they've connected me to some sophisticated device, which enables them to read my thoughts - but that seems improbable. If that were the case, they could have avoided all these complications with communications - skipped over the Morse code, the antenna operation, the hearing-aid glasses, and the lipreading. They cannot read my thoughts. On the other hand, there's a small chance that I can read some of theirs. If I could bone up on my mind reading, I would undeniably be at an advantage. But it's so seldom that anyone comes within range. This morning the research team contented itself with appearing in the doorway and waving. And Emma no longer stays long with Omega. Feeding has been rationed. Emma runs by with little, pre-measured, water-soluble packets. She chucks us what we have coming and disappears.

50

I have made a point by point plan of escape:

1. *Preparations*: The most difficult problem will not be how to get out of the aquarium, but rather, how to stay alive. To keep myself alive, I have to store up glucose and trace elements, zinc above all. If I'm thrifty, I can lay up a store of these substances in my interior hollows, the ventricles as they are called. Since they haven't placed any analyzing instruments in my interior, this should go undetected. They content themselves with testing the fluid in the aquarium and that won't show any variation.

   The Hand will play a decisive role. Thus I have to work on my linking up with the Hand; I have to be in control of every move it makes. I also have to see to it that Omega does not interfere. It ought to work. If I'm not miscalculating, Omega is now at the stage where various treatments have begun to be administered, electric shocks among other things. Thus, Omega ought to be flat on his back for some days.

2. *The security camera*: Those periods of time during which the eye of the camera is directed away from my hood - eleven seconds at most - are too short for large-scale operations. A number of technical preparations are possible, but the escape itself cannot happen so fast. Someone may also be sitting in the surveillance centre and monitoring the camera images. Just because the film goes into a cassette doesn't guarantee that they content themselves solely with scrutinizing it afterwards. But if the escape takes place with a great enough element of

surprise, the security staff will scarcely have time to react. And when they react, their reaction will indirectly facilitate my escape.

3. *Omega*: I have to size up the situation as follows: the idea of our both escaping together is an utterly futile one. If I succeed, it will mean, as a matter of course, that security here in the lab will be tightened; which in turn will make it harder for Omega to get out later. Unfortunately, I see no solution to this problem. But there is one positive factor: if I succeed, I will have shown Omega that one *can* escape. I want to be sure that Omega will not be harmed. Owing to the fact that his aquarium stands 10 centimetres higher than my own, there's a reasonable margin of safety.

4. *The escape*: One suitable night - probably the night before a Monday at 0330 - I will have the Hand get out when the camera is looking away. The Hand will block off the drain that is still here from the emergency shower. Since the camera is installed precisely where the shower once was, it cannot see what is directly underneath it. Thus the Hand can calmly drag over cloth and rags and block up the drain. Then the Hand will turn on the water; there are at least three taps here. There are even tools on a rack on the wall, in case the taps are stuck. Now the water level is rising rapidly in the room. The Hand swims over to my aquarium and disconnects the majority of the plugs. For my own energy consumption I need what's called a sea-battery, a little plastic bag that is activated in water. These sorts of batteries are used all over the institute and can easily be stolen. At the same moment that the water in the room begins to splash into my aquarium, the Hand swims down towards the drain in order to move the rags aside. Now comes the critical moment: if this happens too quickly, the water will stop rising before it has reached a level that will permit me to swim out. If it happens too slowly, the flood will have time to overflow Omega's level; since Omega will not have stored up the necessary chemical substances in advance, he will end up in water that is too dilute and will die.

Now I find myself swimming out into the flooded laboratory. Because there's a whirlpool, I am drawn towards the opened drain. Now the Hand also has to lift aside the cast-iron grate that covers the drain. Once this is done, I can disappear down the pipes with the Hand in tow. We know very little about the life that awaits us there. But we know that there is water, that this water runs through rocky tunnels and concrete canals towards a purifying plant. The water is not clean - which is a considerable advantage. There ought to be quite a lot of nutrients and trace elements, maybe even vitamins. We do not intend to follow the stream all the way to the purifying station. We will sit ourselves down in a suitable niche and plan for our future.

5. *Failure*: If the plan miscarries at any of the critical stages, I will take my own life. Unfortunately it is impossible to plan this out in detail. But with full control of the Hand, it should not be a problem. The worst that can happen is that I get caught in the water en route from my aquarium to the drain. If the escape is interrupted before I have left my nest, it makes less difference. No one can accuse me of trying to escape as long as I'm still lying there in my aquarium. If the Hand does not succeed in removing the heavy grate from the drain, we can count on help from the guard. What does a watchman do when he discovers a flood? He checks out the plumbing. He looks up at his control panel and immediately sees a red lamp lighting up, indicating the block is in the lab. Then he has two alternatives, either he will call the fire department or go himself in high rubber boots into the lab in order to remove the obstacle from the drain. Once the obstacle is gone, the Hand and I will glide down into the hole . . .

Suddenly the professor is standing leaning over me, despite the fact that it is not time for the ordinary rounds:
  - What are you lying there brooding over?
  I prefer not to answer. Instead I think: now or never! I stretch and strain my gaze until it reaches into his brow. He is not so

180

frightfully tanned today, his skin is more like sweaty cheese. I focus on his forehead, penetrate the skin, the envelope of muscles, the bones . . . I command: Take me into your hands!

The professor raises his hands from his coat pockets and stares astonished into his own palms.

I repeat the command: Take me into your hands!

He begins to roll up his sleeves and then takes off his wristwatch. Then he bends forward and begins to move aside the trimmings - the wires, the oxygen pump, the frequency analyzer - in order to reach me. I have to tip all the way backwards now, so as not to lose sight of his forehead . . .

- What the hell am I standing here and doing?!

He takes a hasty step backwards and guiltily hides his hands behind his back. Then he fishes a pair of sunglasses out of his breast pocket and looks at me through dark lenses - as if it were his eyes that he needed to shield.

- Listen now, Ypsilon, don't go trying out any of your tricks on me! We know very well that you can influence other creatures' movements. To a certain degree. In actuality, you are no more remarkable than any two-bit mesmerist!

He takes off the glasses again. He has realized that he has the situation completely under control.

- You are thinking of escaping, he remarks. For several days now we have been noticing in your samples that you are lying here spinning great plans for your escape.

- Yes, I intend to escape.

- Good luck!

- Will you help me?

- I feel honoured by your confidence . . . no, Ypsilon, let us speak man to man: However much I would like to help you, however much I would like to see a good, old friend freed from his physical matter . . . It is not I who own you, you are not my private property! You belong to Biochine. If you want to flee, you will have to do it in your imagination. I cannot stop you from doing that. The most I can do is try to keep track of how you're doing.

- You're a coward.

- No, I am not particularly cowardly. I might even consider committing a breach of trust. I could consider tricking Biochine and taking the consequences, if only for once in my life to get to experience the inconceivable: that someone in your situation *can succeed* in escaping. But, Ypsilon, but . . .

- Let me out!!

- Yes, I will release you. But, unfortunately, not into freedom. It's too late for that. Our plans have already gone much too far. Far too many outsiders are already involved . . . It's already decided that tomorrow you will be moved straight across the lab, to Omega over there.

- Why?!

- Because it's high time you began to get used to close contact with each other.

51

Omega and I are in a long, narrow, glass tank. Between us there is a thin sheet of plastic, which makes bodily contact between us impossible. Over us, a lid of wire netting keeps trespassers from entering. I can no longer see the Hand - but it ought to be on the shelf below us. I have called to it several times, without result.

What would have happened if there had been some hitch in my attempt to escape by flooding the laboratory, if the whole building filled up with water to the attic? Omega would have floated out, of course. What about the rats in the attic? Would they have come swimming with whiplashing tails, through the ventilation system into our lab? Maybe there are other organs in this building? Surely they have hearts, either hanging in aquariums like ours, or frozen alive, under wraps, in dry ice. Big, fat, red-brown livers waiting to be received, and arms, eyes, eardrums, duodena - the human body's entire insides blazing in living colour. If there were a deluge here, they would all be pulled loose: the hearts pumping, the intestines darting along like eels, the lungs pressing up against the ceiling like sponges. We could form a whole body if we got on well. If only we could prevail on someone to sew us together.

The research team enters. No one says a word. The needle on the EEG-machine trembles in the background. After he's made a note of the time, the professor pulls up the plastic barrier that separates me from Omega. What for? A cockfight on the scientific level - or simply an opportunity for us to get used to each other's secretions?

When I first approach him, Omega lies perfectly still; only a few of the nerve fibres on his underside sway weakly. I nose around. Omega has a brown eye. Its various parts are not clearly demarcated; the pupil, the iris, and the white seem to flow together. Maybe his origin is completely different from mine. Indian? Mongolian? I would so like to show him in some way that my intentions are peaceable. But what shall I do? When I come closer I send speech out through one antenna:

- It's me, Ypsilon.

But he doesn't react. He is at an earlier stage of development, at the same level I myself was until quite recently: lipreading and using sign language. I go down towards the bottom so that he will not feel threatened. What's hiding there, deep inside him?

Suddenly Omega darts away like a frightened fish. He does not use his ears to swim; he uses the network of cerebral nerves to propel himself through the water, like a jellyfish; with a couple of powerful pumping strokes he runs right into the short end of the fishtank. I am nearly overturned as a result. I turn around as gently as a galley and point my stem towards Omega. He's pressed himself into a corner with his backside to me; now and then his nerve fibres twitch. He brings to mind a frog attempting to flee under the water line. I cry out into the laboratory:

- George?! Emma?!

No one comes. No one speaks. I cannot even register the presence of bodies either in the laboratory or in the adjacent room. But I am sure that we're being observed.

I go down to the bottom and try to make myself as small and flat as possible. Suddenly Omega takes a leaping bound straight up out of the water. Naturally enough, he rebounds off the aquarium's mesh lid and splashes back down. Like a dead beetle, he sinks, back first, down towards the bottom. There he lies, immobile, but staring wildly. Can Omega turn himself right side up - or does he need help? I let him lie there for about half an hour until he calms down. Then I dare not wait any longer. Omega's entrails may get out of whack; his nuclei may get crushed to pieces, thoughts and images fall out of their pigeonholes and become one huge muddle inside there.

Very carefully I swim nearer and give him a little shove with the stump of my medulla oblongata. When I nudge him, Omega's nerve fibres shake, as if he were groping for something to hold on to. I do not, however, manage to turn him over. I consider whether I should try to tow him to the surface. I come closer again, this time at slightly greater speed, and try to press myself under him, so that I have him on my back and can lift him up. Something smacks against my eye - it feels like I've rammed my skull into the wall. Now I'm stuck. I can't move. Omega is too heavy. Moreover, it seems that one of my antennae is caught in one of Omega's deepest furrows, the sulcus lateralis.

If only I could speak with him! With our combined powers we could certainly get ourselves out of this mess. But one moment he is deaf and dumb; in the next he begins to fight violently, like a drowning person. His long nerve fibres lash my back like whips. Instinctively I cower, and then get my ears going at full speed. It's lucky there's no sand or clay at the bottom of the fishtank - otherwise we'd stir up so much sludge that neither of us would be able to see the other.

Suddenly I come loose and rush away, broadside first. Then I come to a dead stop. Omega's long nerve stems have wrapped themselves several times around my antennae. The harder I struggle, the tighter the knots are pulled. I try to think: if we get stuck in each other, it isn't the end of the world; sooner or later someone has to come and separate us. The important thing is that neither of us lies supine for too long. Omega now seems to have regained his strength; he begins to twist and wrench and go towards his own side of the tank. Presumably he is so completely disorientated that he doesn't know up from down. I get pulled along and let him drag me across the bottom. He is still lying on his back like a helpless turtle; all his strength seems to lie in the long towrope of nerves. He suddenly makes a 90-degree turn and I dash over and past him, towards the other end of the aquarium. I begin to swim as if possessed, in order to get the situation under control and to keep myself on an even keel. Omega has now turned again and struggles back towards the place where we first got tangled up with each other. I summon up all the strength I have - but I must now fully realize that Omega is the stronger. He is also heavier. Strangely enough, for his volume is less than mine. It's patently clear that he has a higher specific weight. I choose another tactic: to let him tire himself out. But he has unsuspected endurance. For several hours he drives back and forth over the bottom with his belly up in the air and me in tow. I begin to feel seasick. If my organs of equilibrium get upset, I myself can land in a perilous, life-threatening, supine position. For a moment I think: why not? Why not prepare to die now? I haven't any future anyhow. Old recollections wash in over my consciousness. I think of Emma, slender and pretty. How I could lie for days and days and try to figure out a way to declare my love to her. I remember my old contempt for the professor, something I can no longer afford.

Omega makes an unexpected pumping motion, shoots up obliquely from the bottom, touches a wall, and ricochets up above the water surface. I follow with no possibility of braking. When we plop back into the water, he is lying on top of me, still upside down. I myself am in a lateral position, but am kept from capsizing by his nerve fibres, now infinitely coiled and looped around me. We are both all tired out. If I try to turn Omega upright, I myself will land belly up. I lie still and make small, tired, irregular strokes with my outer ears, to cool us off a little at least.

I believe that we lie like this for some 24 hours, without food, without care. I make one attempt to send emergency signals via my antennae, but doubtless this is vain; I am lying in Omega's radio shadow, underneath him. For long periods of time I am somewhere else. Only later do I begin to wonder why we are not sinking. My specific weight is such that my resting position is just about halfway between top and bottom. Omega is more compact. According to all natural laws, we ought to sink to the bottom. There seems to be only one explanation why we don't: Omega is dead.

I repress this fact at once and try to sleep. When I wake up again, his eye-stalk is crooked. The heavy eye hangs down bent in front of me. Without any great hope, I swim a few strokes. To my surprise and relief I feel how I am being released from his grasp; his nerves are slippery, cold, and as lifeless as overcooked spaghetti. After a bit of wheedling and eeling around, I come entirely free. Immediately I swim away and press against the bottom as far away from Omega as I can get. Is he dead? When he begins to dissolve and poison the water, will I also die? Decomposition is sure to begin within a few hours; after all, the water we are resting in is at body temperature.

But after only a few minutes the psychiatrist comes and slides down the plastic barrier between us. She gives Omega an injection in his longitudinal fissure, the one between his two hemispheres. In the afternoon he is his old self: lying and glaring at me with his spherical eye. I no longer have the energy to make any attempt at contact. Why did he attack me? Do I, wholly unconsciously, release aggressive transmitter-substances into the surrounding fluid?

52

Now, tonight, I must attempt to escape; it *has to* succeed. Something's up here: extra rounds, new equipment, calibrations, and visits from management. Something is going to happen. I have an instinctive feeling that it will change my whole life, perhaps as radically as when they lifted me out of my own body. I must get away tonight. Cost what it may.

As often happens when complicated tasks must be accomplished in a short period of time, careless mistakes are made. After giving the Hand its injection yesterday, Emma did not see to it that the lid of its aquarium was securely locked into position. The Hand is already out now. It is on its way to the locker room, where Curt's soiled coat hangs - the one he stuffed under the plank bed in anger when he left the institute. The cleaning woman has hung it up on a hook. In the pocket of the coat is the long TV cable Curt used when he connected me to the surveillance camera.

The Hand comes slithering up against the wall, while the camera stares in the wrong direction, off towards my old hood on the other side of the room. The Hand stumbles along like a lunar module the last bit of the way, until it is under the camera, in its eye's blind spot. The TV cord is rolled up but not knotted. The Hand unwinds the coil and fingers its way up, holding one end of the cord towards the camera. But it doesn't stick the plug into it just yet. Instead, I let the Hand loosely fasten the cord around the base of the camera - then I let it climb down.

Omega lies there, staring wide-eyed. Be my guest! As long as Omega cannot report on his observations, it almost feels reassuring to have a spectator. The Hand cannot budge the metal net that covers our long, divided aquarium. But there's no need for it to. All the Hand has to do is guide the other end of the cord through the opening in the net that surrounds the oxygen pump. I press myself close up against the gleaming pole, where oxygen spurts out through tiny holes and rolls its way up to the water surface in oval bubbles of increasing size. The Hand inserts its index and middle fingers. I take aim and drive my blind optic nerve stem right into the cord's metal cap.

The Hand lets go of the cap. In less than a minute the Hand is up on the camera again, tearing out the ordinary connection and plugging me in. The black and white field of vision flares up in my consciousness: now I see the laboratory obliquely from above in long, sweeping glances.

All my energy and concentration are focussed on moving my consciousness from the aquarium to the camera. Hardest of all is to entirely disconnect my own, colour-seeing eye. Periodically images from the aquarium break through: rolling, gilded bubbles of oxygen in the faintly green water. But the picture grows weaker and weaker until it fades, like an old water-colour. Finally it is nothing more than a light, trembling fleck.

I leave my sense of sight and concentrate on other parts of my being: hearing creeps slowly, like the spark along the fuse up in the camera. Various fantasies, recollections, and bits of knowledge follow. I mine the quarry of the Island of the Apes, the woman in black who sits beside the respirator, the dog, the rats who padded in so discreetly one night so long ago . . . Finally my consciousness has almost completely gone up into the camera. If I'd had the time I would have done some screening. I would have left all the negative things behind. Emma slips away too - that's all right, as long as I get out of here.

Now comes the next step: I have to get the Hand to unplug me from my old brain and patch me into the main cable system instead. Through it I intend to stream on through the lines to the TV panel in the surveillance room. I cannot foresee what awaits me there: maybe I'll wind up in a video cassette and lie for months in some desk drawer before they play me. Then I can make my next leap: either penetrate the forehead of whoever is sitting in front of the screen, or whiz past and whir out into the blue like a tightly packed swarm of bees.

I search for the Hand with my gaze in order to issue my final instructions. But when I sweep over the laboratory I see something else. I've been so busy that I haven't noticed the professor and the psychiatrist. They are standing roughly in the middle of the floor and waving cheerfully. Both of them are in evening dress: the professor in tails, the lanky psychiatrist in a long dress and with a light fur cape over her shoulders. The professor has the Hand on his arm, which he fondles like a kitten.

– Crawl back into your shell, snail! the professor says sternly, but suddenly bursts out cackling.

Raising his free arm toward me in a grandiose gesture, the professor recites something from the *Odyssey*:

> *Noble Laertes' Son, inventive Odysseus,*
> *so now you want to go home, to the beloved*
> *soil of your fathers. Fare you well then, go*
> *with my blessing. But if you knew in your soul*
> *how many trials you must endure before you reach*
> *that land, you would stay here in the grotto with me*
> *always, and with me be immortal . . .*

53

Now they are making renovations again. They have knocked down the wall opposite me, the one against which my former hood was placed. A jagged hole with sharp edges is in the centre of my field of vision: brown, bowed, reinforcing bars stick out; bent pipes project like periscopes - from the ceiling dangle loose cables with fluttering insulating tape. Everywhere dust is falling. They have wheeled in a vacuum cleaner with accordion-pleated hoses, thick as thighs. Every water surface vibrates.

A room big as a public swimming hall opens on the other side of the torn-down wall. The ceiling is vaulted, as in a railway station. The ceiling's oblong windows are covered over with white fabric. The whole floor is broken up. Dust-covered men cut moulds. Constructions that look like staircases rise up towards the hall's far wall. The whole business looks like a huge stage. What are they going to put on, *Götterdämmerung*?

Four flour-covered figures stride in through the hole in the wall. When they come nearer, I see that they are not workers. They are an amplified research team, in white from top to toe. But they are not, as usual, led by the professor. Ahead of the professor, the psychiatrist, and an unfamiliar person, walks a solid, bald-headed, authoritative man. His polished, freckled crown is surrounded by thin, straggly wisps of angel's hair. He is old, 70 at least. His face is heavy, his eyelids as thick as lips. He doesn't move a muscle in his face, except for his nostrils. His nostrils are big, square, and wide-open with curiosity. But his cornflower-blue eyes seem to sleep under the blanket of their lids. They stop a few metres away from us. The professor is showing X-rays. The old man mutters so that I can't hear what he is saying. But I can hear the professor and the psychiatrist; they are speaking schoolbook German.

Now they are looking through medical records. They must be Omega's since mine have been stolen. They're also surveying long EEG-curves and they pluck out some multicoloured sheets with lab-test results. Then they all leave suddenly, all but the fourth person, a younger man with a stethoscope in his breast pocket. He bends down over Omega.

- Who are you? I ask.
- The anaesthesiologist.
- And the old boy who left, the authoritative one?
- Best neurosurgeon in the world, he says, without irony.
- Are you going to give Omega an antenna operation?

He doesn't answer, just shakes his head as one does when one must deal with someone who is ignorant. Instead, he sucks up a little of our water in a pipette, holds the pipette towards the light from the window, and peers at it. Are we feeling well? He places the pipette in a round bowl beside the aquarium, and instead begins to poke at Omega with a spatula.

There doesn't seem to be any question that they are preparing to perform an operation. My guess is that it's an antenna operation. That ought to be it, if they're having Omega follow the same programme I did. It would be less lonely for me if I could talk with Omega. We haven't said a word to each other in weeks. The Hand has also vanished since I last saw it resting in the crook of George's arm.

Now the anaesthesiologist drains the water from Omega's half of the aquarium. This does not affect me because the plastic barrier between us is down. When Omega places himself at the bottom and the water sinks around him, he changes form. Once all the water is gone he flattens out from his own weight; his resemblance to an egg disappears. Instead, he suggests an inflated blowfish.

192

The surgical team wheels in a high lab-cart, which is bedded with compresses and sheets. The dried-off Omega is carefully lifted over on to the lab-cart. They roll out with the anaesthesiologist in tow. I turn my attention once again to the room that looks like a swimming hall. A crane has been brought in. In the basket of the crane - which shoots up towards the ceiling on a gleaming telescopic tube - stand two men who attach long poles to the ceiling. Long fixtures for fluorescent tubes are suspended from the poles, and these lights hang almost all the way down to the floor.

The surgical team with the lab-cart is suddenly visible again. They carefully lift the lab-cart up over the pleated hoses of the vacuum cleaner. Are they already through with Omega? A new world record in that case. Can that indolent old man really perform an antenna operation in five minutes? Or has something happened - has Omega suddenly begun to feel ill, or has someone thrown sand into the sterilized operating equipment?

The anaesthesiologist comes back too. Omega is probably still drugged, and great care must be taken when they put him back into the aquarium. But the anaesthesiologist turns his back on the lab-cart. Instead, he bends down over me and slowly begins to raise the plastic barrier. Immediately my water gushes over into Omega's empty compartment, and then runs out through the valve in the bottom. I sink, as between the steep walls of a lock in a canal. Before my eye is pinched by the weight of my own cerebrum, I see that the lab-cart is empty. Omega is not en route back. Instead, it is my turn.

54

- Are we awake now?

About a dozen people are standing around us. All of them sport turquoise overalls. Over their mouths they wear small, muzzle-like masks that resemble paper cups but are of moulded cardboard. Nonetheless, their voices are distinctly audible. One is a doctor. He stands farthest forward and scratches his head with an electronic stethoscope. His turquoise cap almost meets his eyebrows. Still, it is evident that he is smiling. The corners of his eyes glitter with laughter lines. Obliquely behind him stands a nurse who clasps a looseleaf binder to her bosom. The others look on wide-eyed but maintain a certain distance.

- Cheer up! says the doctor.

The research team walks across the room. A couple of them bend down - over what? Then they go over to the window and look outside.

- Well, winter is over now, in any case, the doctor says.

The research team marches out to the left. A bed stands directly opposite. In the bed an older man sits up halfway. His eyes are half-closed. A thin rubber tube is inserted in one of his nostrils; it goes in an arc to his cheek, where it is taped fast. From there the tube runs down off the bed. On the man's bare breast, several thin wires of various colours are fastened. These wires gather into a bunch, which leads to an oscilloscope up above the man's head. In the oscilloscope's window the man's heart beats. His hands are bound with gauze to the bedposts - not tightly; one hand picks and pokes at the sheet. The other one, blue-red and swollen, lies completely still. At the foot of the bed there's a metal rack, not unlike a TV aerial. Plastic bags filled with fluids hang in the ribs of the rack. All the fluids are the colour of water except for the one which is a furious red-yellow, like picric acid. Slender tubes run to a box down at the base of the rack. From there a somewhat thicker tube leads to one of the man's feet. He has a pillow between his feet.

A woman with a wide turquoise coat over her clothes comes in from the left. First she walks towards the bed of the man who is half-sitting; but she stops herself and turns right. In one hand she has a bouquet of coltsfoot. The stems are wrapped in aluminium foil. She takes a chair and sits down.

- How does it feel to lie in Intensive Care?

It is Emma. She is looking for some place to stash the flowers, but can't find anything.

- The first flowers of the year! she says, inhaling their scent.

She sits a while but begins to fidget. When the man opposite begins to wheeze, she turns around. Then she looks at the clock. She rises and extends a half-open hand, as you might do if you wanted to touch someone's cheek. But her hand stops halfway.

- I'm afraid I have to be off.

She waves and leaves. She still doesn't know where to put the flowers. She takes them with her.

The image of the room and the man in the bed pales and becomes grainy. The curves lose their sharpness. Grey glides over into black and then into snow-white.

- Good evening, Cortex!

It is the professor. He is not wearing turquoise clothing, but rather his good old white lab coat. His mask covers only his chin.

- Can we hear one another? Good . . .

Then he holds up a piece of cardboard, which reads CORTEX.

- Read!
- Cortex.

- That's right. Good. Your new name is Cortex.
- Our new name is Cortex.

He puts the sign on a chair and comes closer.

- Everything has gone better than we'd dreamed, he says. Now for a short briefing: the operation that took place yesterday went off without a hitch. It took scarcely half the estimated eighteen hours. A *feat*, Cortex! All your vital signs are fine. How's your field of vision? Not seeing double are you?
- Certainly not.
- *Good*. Actually, we thought it would take some time. I have never before seen flesh that healed so quickly. Would you say your new name again, just as a check?
- Cortex.
- Cortex means bark, brain-bark in this case. Ingenious, eh? We thought it up ourselves. The language lab had half a year to work on it, and the day before yesterday we asked: have you come up with a new name for Ypsilon and Omega? And what do they reply? 'We need longer to think about it.' Thanks, I said, but in that case we'll have to solve the problem ourselves. The operation itself takes place tomorrow. How are you feeling: sad or happy?
- We don't understand the question.
- Good. We see that in your readings too. Now, where were we? The briefing: well, what can one say . . . Quite simply, we sewed you together. First we divided you, separated each of your two hemispheres. Then we took Ypsilon's left one and sewed it together with Omega's right one. And since Omega is left-handed, his right half functions as a left half. Now we have *two* left halves. For the first time in the history of science! Let me tell you: our worst problem until now was to get hold of a left-handed donor. It took more than normal luck.

Suddenly he falls silent and takes a few steps backward:

- Cortex, let me be honest: you almost frighten me. Who is it I am speaking to? A doubled intellect with no feelings. Chills start to run up the base of one's spine.
- Will you go on playing the cello for us?

- No, Cortex. You can forget about music . . . Do you feel deprived?
- Deprived?
- You don't understand the question? Of course not. A week from now you can go home. If the renovations are done. But that will take care of itself. In a little while, I'll be meeting the board of directors at a small luncheon. Don't worry, Cortex! The first time in the history of neurophysiology! The grant checks will stream into the mailbox like Christmas cards. Is there anything else you're wondering about?
- The question is irrelevant. The answer is no.
- You sound like a computer that has been preprogrammed with questions and answers. But don't you ever forget it, Cortex: you are no computer! You are something infinitely more complicated: a functioning double intellect. Anything else you're wanting . . . No, dumb question. Instead, I'll say: can I do something for you?
- We want to play chess.
- Of course, it must be damned boring to just lie here. And in this company . . .
He gives a hasty glance at the old man, who is sitting halfway up. Then he gets a pad and pencil:
- Chess. Microcomputerized, or the old kind with wooden men?
- We cannot move wooden pieces. We want a modern one, whose squares light up and go out.
- With a computerized opponent?
- What use have we of a computer? We have each other.
He laughs and writes. Then he extends his fist to shake hands, but stops himself and takes his own hand. With a solemn expression, he gives himself a brief, firm handshake.

55

The process of imprinting takes place as described below. Foetuses between the ages of 8 and 12 weeks - all the result of legal abortions - are transferred to the laboratory. Foetuses under 8 weeks are not used because they cannot survive the adjustment; those over 12 weeks are not used for legal reasons. Each foetus is placed in a glass chamber, the top of which is a plate with a hole whose size can vary. The foetus's diminutive body is lowered through the hole, the foetus's skull remains above it. The dividing line is the auditory meatus.

After each foetus has been placed in a chamber which has a skull-hole of appropriate size, the brain is laid bare by means of a circular incision above the auditory meatus and eyes. The membranes of the brain are left intact. Once the skull-cap has been removed, each brain can grow freely. The body, however, is allowed to grow only to a certain size: no more than 13 centimetres from the seventh cervical vertebra to the heels. If the body is allowed to grow longer than 13 centimetres, it puts too great a strain on the circulatory system. A foetus less than 13 centimetres in length, on the other hand, has too small a heart in relation to the swelling brain. The heart of the foetus must at least correspond in size to that of a mouse. Smaller hearts can, indeed, supply the growing brain with blood for a certain period of time; but then the pulse exceeds 160 beats per minute, which is considered the critical cut-off point.

The foetuses rest in fluid. Each chamber is hermetically sealed off from the one next to it. The fluid supplies neither oxygen nor nourishment; it keeps the foetus from desiccating and acts as an effective shock-absorber. Oxygen and nourishment are pumped through the foetus's own circulatory system. However, the blood is not oxygenated via the lungs; they are too under-developed. Each foetus is connected, via its umbilical cord and placenta, to a lung machine.

Normally, the weight of the foetus brain doubles in 22 days. When it has reached a weight of 600 grams, growth is inter-rupted by the addition of hormones. The exposed brain of a finished foetus is the size of a grapefruit; it has a diameter of 13 centimetres, i.e., the same length as the body of the foetus down to its heels. If the brain is permitted to grow larger, the blood supply becomes insufficient. With the exception of the lungs, the foetus's organs are, to all intents and purposes, entirely self-supporting. The sense organs - eyes, ears, etcetera - nevertheless remain undeveloped. The same is true of all muscles but the heart. The kidneys, too, are among those few organs which do not function. Thus, in addition to the lung machine, each foetus is equipped with an artificial kidney. The whole system is closed; should the chemical composition within it be disturbed, it can normally be adjusted via the lung or kidney machines.

The anatomy of the foetus brain distinguishes itself from that of brains grown in the womb. The folding of the cerebrum is less marked. The foetus brains can also take on relatively diverse forms, with no effect on brain function. Some brains are globular, others are oviform, while a few may assume the shape of a head of cauliflower or that of a trumpet mushroom.

The actual aim of the breeding is to control the *internal* development of the foetus brains. By suppressing the internal development of the right hemisphere, brains with two left halves are produced. Functionally speaking, that is. Close examination, however, will reveal the longitudinal fissure and the traditional left and right hemispheres respectively. The brain of a growing foetus follows the pattern of its mother's brain. If the mother's brain is lacking - as in the present cases - the matrix of another adult brain can be substituted. This is where we come in.

The fluid-filled, cubiform incubators with their foetuses suspended from transverse plates are divided from one another by a system of locks. A lock, quite simply, is a fluid-filled cube with no foetus inside it. The locks are essential; they enable us to pass from one foetus to the next, without the various foetuses' fluids coming into direct contact with one another. The entire process must be carried out under sterile conditions. Without the intervening locks, the entire colony of foetuses would quickly be infected if but one microorganism took hold in a single foetus. The growing brains are extremely susceptible to infection.

Usually we remain with a foetus for 96 hours. This is the optimal period of time needed to 'transfer' our pattern to the foetus. Then we swim on, through the locks, to the next foetus. The transferring, or imprinting, must be repeated after 22 days. Thus, we can service five growing foetuses in parallel. Two days remain for recovery and adjustments. We spend these two days in our old aquarium in the little laboratory. Normally the foetus brain reaches its ideal weight of 600 grams in 14 weeks. After the 'major overhaul' we begin a new round.

The finished foetus brains are transferred to cocoons, as they are called here. These cocoons are of metal, about one metre high, 30 centimetres wide, and 50 centimetres long. Each cocoon contains all that is needed to support the brain: a mechanical lung, a mechanical kidney, a heating line, control instruments, etcetera. The cocoons come in different constructions and sizes. In one model, the small vestigial body below the brain is retained, and the foetus's own heart continues to pump, just as during the growth period. In others, the body is amputated, and the brain rests directly in a nutrient solution. In other models, the brain itself is imbedded in a sterile gelatin, or in compressed oxygen.

The customers' requirements determine what sort of cocoon is used. Because brain tissue is relatively insensitive to ionized radiation, the atomic industry - both military and civilian - is a big customer. If the radiation is extreme, the brain can be placed in quicksilver. On the other hand, the space industry's prime requirement is shock-resistance. Owing to its elasticity, the brain in its natural condition is not particularly sensitive to physical shock; but in the context of outer space, it may become essential to provide intricate hydraulic safety systems. The majority of brains, however, have stationary applications within various spheres of industry and research. Here the only problem to contend with is maintaining sterile conditions. These clients generally have wide experience with advanced computers and their care and maintenance. However, they have no experience with prophylactic devices, and starting up the requisite facilities initially caused difficulties.

In the fiscal year just ended, the production of individual foetus brains was Biochine's most profitable sector. We are still alone in the market. Our technological headstart has caused difficulties for wide sectors of the conventional information technology industry. This decline is partly psychologically determined. As always, when a technological breakthrough is made, the market suffers a shock: the old techniques are thought to be totally obsolete. Such pessimism is seldom wholly warranted. After some time has passed, new market niches can be found for the old techniques, in the developing countries for example. That Biochine has been able cheaply to buy up its competitors should also be factored into our profitability, for soon they will show a profit on their old products.

56

We're in the aquarium, or in the garage, as George says. The glass portal that leads to the breeder is closed. The ceiling light is out. Out there in the big, dusky hall, several people in sterile attire work at changing foetuses. The lab workers wear light-coloured overalls and plastic hats like miners' helmets. Once they have lifted out the fully grown foetuses, they will insert the new ones. Then a new generation will begin to grow. After 14 weeks they will change them again. The completely grown foetuses have bodies as pale as roots. The swollen, unconfined brains assume different colours of the spectrum: pink - light-red - blazing-red - purple - violet. They shine like faint lanterns. When asleep, they are dark from the blood in their veins; when they awaken the colour lightens. If one sets them a task, the brains flicker and flare angrily in the semi-darkness.

We have gone through the usual 14-weeks' major overhaul with nothing to complain of. Minor tune-ups go on from every 20th to 22nd day; we lie here during those intervals. While they exchange foetuses, as they are doing now, and sterilize the basins for the new generation, we are free for a whole week. We have nothing to do when we are free. We would very much like to waive this recess. We have also suggested they utilize our capacity in some other way while we are lying here. But our employers have trouble enough keeping up with us, even more difficulty thinking up something new. Logically, it would be best if we also supervised the working process in general, if we became our own employers. The people all around us are severely handicapped.

A woman sits down in the operator's chair obliquely in front of us. It is Emma. We know all about her. She stopped working here some time ago. She suffered emotional disturbances from the work here. We look at her out of our left eye; our right eye remains fixed on the foetus exchange.

- I'll never learn . . . Emma says. I still want to say Ypsilon or Omega.

- Call us what you will. In any case we know who you mean.

- Yes, I thought to ask you, Ypsilon, you wouldn't by any chance want to move in with me . . . When you are no longer needed here, I mean?

- We are needed here.

- That can come to an end.

- Let us suppose that it comes to an end, we say. What exactly, concretely speaking, does your invitation imply?

- Nowadays I work in an Extended Care Ward. Most of the patients have been in respirators for years. I thought that . . .

- . . . we should move there. Why?

- Well, someone has to take care of you, if things end here. I want to take care of you. I don't want to see you end up like your right halves, those which were left over after they sewed you together. They took the opportunity to sew up your right halves then, too. Did you know that?

- Why shouldn't we know that?

- Then you also know that Biochine donated you . . . I mean half of you two . . . to Stanford University in California? To a schizophrenia research laboratory. They're testing out all sorts of medicines and new methods of treatment on your . . . twin? Is that what one should call it?

- Not a twin. We no longer have anything in common. We are Cortex. The others, those 'right brains', are called Id, which means the unconscious. We've had a short briefing from the professor. Id looks like an amoeba.

- I don't want Biochine to donate you to a research lab when you're not needed here!

- Why not? It might interest us.

Tears run down her cheeks while her mouth smiles. We know what this means: she is sad but does not want to upset us. But when we try to put ourselves in Emma's place, to find out how she 'feels' - then we instantly become sleepy. When one is incapable of engaging oneself, nothing but sleep - in the broader sense of the word - remains. We fill in our amputated domains with sleep.

We are awakened by her standing there and screaming:

- Once I loved you, Ypsilon!

- We have heard something quite different from Curt, the post-doctoral student. He said that you felt like vomiting whenever you were forced to handle us.

- That *schmuck*!

She thumps down in the chair with her face in her hands. Once again an overpowering sleepiness smites us. When we get sleepy, we automatically tip backward, so that our glance is aimed at the ceiling.

- I love you even though you no longer have the slightest possibility of understanding what I mean.

- Do not underestimate us. We do understand. We understand everything, more or less as an experienced physician understands his patients. But do not ask that we cry too.

Now they are done out there in the big hall. The last foetus, naked and marzipan-coloured like a newborn kitten, is planted in its fluid-filled cube. In a few minutes the glass portal will be raised and we can swim into the locks for a new period of work. When we think about the new generation of foetuses we will imprint during the next 14 weeks, our somnolence vanishes instantly.

Emma holds one of her hands in front of her face. With the other she tentatively gropes towards the glass. Again we are smitten with somnolence, as if someone had strewn crushed ice in our convolutions. But then the lamp alongside the glass door blinks green. The portal is raised and with frisky ear-strokes we row into the system.

57

The generations of foetuses are not designated by letters of the Greek alphabet. In accordance with the Latin they are called A, B, C, etcetera. Now we are in cube J:2. The 'spuds', as the new ones are called, become smaller and smaller. J:2 cannot be more than five weeks. Although they are visible to the naked eye, they are hard to work with. To imprint them, we have to place ourselves behind each exposed foetus brain; then, trailing our cerebral nerves, we climb slowly up over it. To the uninitiated, this must look like copulation. There is no problem with larger foetuses. But when the foetus brain is only five weeks, a special directional instrument must be inserted into the cube. This device resembles a bombsight; it consists of a thin sheet of plastic with concentric rings and a cross. In the centre there is a hole the size of a pea for the head of the foetus. The distance between successive rings is ten millimetres. This enables us to position ourselves with precision.

The 14-week periods were reduced at first to 12 weeks and now are down to nine. The tune-up periods have also become shorter - which makes no difference to us; we prefer working to resting. When we leave cube J:2, we encounter yet another change: J:3 is empty. Nothing like this has ever happened before. The foetuses have always been in series. If one of them died, a replacement was made at once. Not so now. We lie in the empty cube and look. It's like being in a hall of mirrors: the same pattern of cubes repeats itself as far as we are capable of seeing.

In the afternoon we proceed to J:4. Here, there is a foetus; but it is so immature that its skull-cap could not be cut away. If the foetuses are too young, there is not even a rudimentary skull-cap to remove. Thus, we move to one side of the foetus and bide our time.

Later, we receive orders to sluice along to J:5. At first we experience the cube as empty. Then we discover a hanging foetus-body with no brain. We sound the alarm at once. This is purely a security measure. They would scarcely leave a dead foetus-body in here - but *if* this one is dead, we have to get out of here immediately.

On those few prior occasions when we have set off the alarm, the staff has appeared within 30 seconds; now it takes 18 minutes before anyone so much as bothers to open the lock. What is the meaning of this? Equipment failure or human error? We do not have access to the information we would require to decide the matter. The next cube we swim over to is unlabelled and empty. This is as it should be, since it is sixth in the row. When we have reached number six, a side-sluice is opened and we swim through a transit shaft that leads us back to J:1.

J:1 is empty. When we were here two weeks ago everything was normal. We assume that J:1 has died, become a 'dud' as they say here. We give the signal to be sluiced to J:2. This goes off normally. But J:2 is empty. No more than ten hours have gone by since we were here last - the shortest rotation period we have experienced. We immediately go on to J:3, which we know is empty. In J:4 the brainless foetus body hangs like a pale beansprout. Now we are entirely certain it is dead. We trigger the alarm at once again. This time the whole night goes by before anyone pays any attention to us.

Early in the morning the ceiling of cube J:4 is opened, which should only take place in emergency situations. A net bag is lowered into the cube. Someone lifts us out in the net and runs us back to the 'garage', that is to say, our resting aquarium in the little laboratory. We are brusquely dropped down into the tank. The person who is responsible for us does not answer our signal. But he bends down and looks at us once we are lying in the aquarium. Above the nameplate on his overall, it no longer reads Biochine; it reads: Cerebro.

58

He has aged noticeably. We remember the professor as a vital man of sixty. Now he is drawn and yellow. In the past, he rarely sat down during the rounds. Now he slumps in a chair. The name Cerebro is on his jacket too.

- Why have you changed nametags? And why can't we work?
- I don't want to talk about it . . . I would much rather have taken my cello along and played for you. But there's no point when you have no . . .
- . . . no right brain, no.
- The old Biochine has been swallowed up by a new cartel, Cerebro. That's all there is to tell.
- It makes no difference to us whether our products carry the label of Biochine or Cerebro. We want to work.
- Too bad, Cortex. Foetus imprinting has come to an end. The technology we used is no longer viable. Imprinting has just proved to be too damned expensive. Yes, we tried all sorts of things. We took younger and younger foetuses, experimented with shorter and shorter periods of time. The financial planners forced us to! But there could be only one result: product quality declined.
- Have we become old-fashioned?
- You have been made obsolete by technological advances. Cell research and genetic engineering have had their great break-throughs. The functions we once needed a whole brain for can now be extracted from a so-called 'honeycomb'. Each comb is a formation of hexagonal cellulose cells. Comb is an inappropriate

term, but since it has proven commercially acceptable, it is used. Actually, it is a very thin, almost transparent film of layers of cells. To attain the same capacity as you have, a closely packed film of cells need be no larger than a fingernail. Even if you consist of two left brains, you drag around a lot of dead weight we did not dare to remove. But the honeycombs don't carry around anything unnecessary. They consist of pure and sheer intelligence.

- But, in any case, we have a capacity of twice 600 IQ.
- Yes. But a comb the size of a postage stamp ranges up toward 1,500. And the largest ones yet created, with roughly the surface area of a credit card, attain a capacity of nearly 10,000 IQ. That's as much intelligence as at a full session of an Academy of Sciences! Nor are they susceptible to infection. Viruses and bacteria don't like cellulose. Possibly, mushrooms could grow on them; but mushrooms grow very slowly. If a comb gets contaminated, the cheapest thing to do is trade it in for a new one. A small honeycomb costs no more than a sparking plug. And who repairs sparking plugs? No, Cortex, your days of glory were splendid but short. Such is life. Myself, I'm not bitter; soon I will retire. But I feel sorry for the faithful old servants, those who cannot be retrained.
- Will we also be retrained?
- No, Cortex, we will leave you in peace . . .
- We have a standing invitation from Emma. She said we could come to the nursing home where she works.
- But you need intensive care.
- It is a respirator ward.
- And who's going to pay for it, the National Health Plan?
- Perhaps the matter could be investigated?
- I am disappointed in you, Cortex. What sort of emotional slop is that . . . extended care! What do you know about life in an extended care ward? What would you do with yourself?
- Perhaps we could play chess with the patients.
- Pardon me if I smile. Noughts and crosses possibly . . . No, I have a better invitation for you. I have in fact managed to do

something I actually never believed possible. No one on the board of directors thought it possible either. I have succeeded in getting you a place in a really fine institution. Actually, I had hoped to be able to go there myself - do you remember what I once told you about, what I told Ypsilon about? About the greatest honour that can be bestowed upon a brain researcher? Do you remember Paul Broca?

- There is nothing wrong with our memory.

- Then I don't need to go into the whole story again. Of course it was a stupid dream. That I should be worthy of being placed on the same shelf as Broca's brain. I will not permit you to laugh at me. Every human being has the right to dream!

- Are we going to Paris?

- You are going to Paris.

- And who is paying for it?

- I am. Out of my own pocket. I do so with pleasure. This very evening you and I will fly to Paris. And go directly to the Musée de l'Homme. A short ceremony will be held when you are installed alongside Broca. In spite of everything, you are the world's first isolated, living human brain.

- But if extended care would be boring . . . how will things be in the Musée de l'Homme?

- Boring? On the same shelf as Broca! I would . . . No, yes! I am jealous. Why shouldn't I admit it. Every scientist, yes, every human being, wants to be immortal! Let us admit it. But I will be forgotten. When I'm dead, I can only hope that my writings will live on in medical libraries the world over . . . As long as it lasts! Did you know that they've begun a clean-up? The quantity of information, quite simply, has become too large. Not owing to space; after all, there are microfilms and micro-memories. But for economic reasons! All that is being kept is what is absolutely necessary for future research. For that matter, this is but one application for the 'honeycombs'. A comb can comb through an entire library in just a few weeks' time! Most things are being dumped.

- We have no sentiments regarding 'immortality'. Purely

intellectually, of course we understand. But we have no emotionally loaded aspirations. We will be happy to resign our place to you.

- Thanks for your concern. But that is out of the question. It is you, not me, the museum has accepted in writing. The French wouldn't want to have a foreign scientist next to Broca. With you though, it is something else again. You can be accepted as an international figure. It is you who will lie in formalin beside Broca.

- In formalin?

- Broca is in formalin.

- So we don't get to take our own aquarium with us? With the immersion heater and the oxygen pump . . . Who will feed us?

- Don't worry. The museum has its treasures very well-insured.

- If we are placed in formalin we will be terminated.

- Let us say that you will cross over into another form of existence. What do we really know about the life after this one? What do we know about what may be going on inside Paul Broca's brain, even though it is in formalin? I hope he's lying there, smiling at us. Even though we can't perceive it.

- We have no feelings vis-à-vis death.

- Good. I had not expected any false sentimentality. To become immortal, after all, really requires that one first be . . . well, yes, dead.

His bony, yellow, old man's hand waves to us, and he gets up. The professor bends down over the aquarium. What happens when the lamp in our skull-cap is extinguished? Will it become pitch-black, or will it be